*For those who know that the Savior Jesus Christ
pursues us through both mystery and romance.*

Galilee gallivant.

Miller, Nelson.

Crown Management, LLC – May 2024

1527 Pineridge Drive
Grand Haven, MI 49417
USA

ISBN-13: 979-8-89292-862-5

1

"And so, we meet again!" Helena greeted Moore at their airliner gate at the Chicago airport.

Helena had been the first to arrive at the gate. She sat where she could see other passengers approaching up the terminal hallway. She had waved to Moore at her first sight of him, before rising to greet him.

Moore smiled the broadest smile in response to Helena's greeting. Yet he found himself oddly speechless. He had been so focused on whether to offer Helena a handshake or hug that no words issued from his open mouth.

Helena rescued Moore, reaching both arms forward in a light but warm and welcoming hug.

"Cat got your tongue, huh?" Helena laughed as they leaned back from their hug.

"Well, you got my tongue," Moore laughed in reply.

Helena smiled warmly in response while still looking in Moore's eyes, giving Moore cause to believe that his impromptu response had conveyed more of his feelings more accurately than any words he might have planned.

Moore resolved on the spot to let his intuitive, right-brain side govern his interactions with Helena during their upcoming trip. He had noticed how poorly his grasping, overly analytic, left-brain side served him, especially in sensitive relationships that required the subtlest reading of signals. And Moore knew he had no more sensitive and significant relationship than his relationship with Helena.

Moore and Helena had met on a prior Holy Lands trip, Moore the widowed pastor and Israel tour guide, Helena the divorced mother of a twenty-something daughter who had come along for that trip. The beauty, inspiration, and surprising drama of that trip had drawn Moore and Helena together, when neither had been looking for a relationship. Each had taken years to recover from their different losses, Moore of a beloved wife, Helena of a philandering husband. Neither had sought a new companion. Yet each had smitten the other in ways that the other was reluctant to admit.

An elderly couple who had been along for that trip, as Moore's longtime friends and supporters, had seen the sparks between Moore and Helena. They had also believed that Moore and Helena were too young to live the rest of their lives without a companion. And so several months after the trip had concluded, with no further contact between Helena and Moore, the elderly couple had separately invited each of them to their house, ostensibly to consider another Holy Lands trip. Their real purpose had been to bring Moore and Helena together again.

The elderly couple's ploy had worked, but only to a point. Moore and Helena had instantly rekindled their flame. But how were a pastor living in one city and a divorcee living in another city to begin a proper relationship? Neither Moore nor Helena had any interest in taking any action that could appear to anyone to be scandalous.

For a time, Helena and Moore kept up contact. Several times, Moore had taken a day to visit Helena, to take her to dinner. They had also twice met for meals and walks at convenient locations between their two cities.

Their times together confirmed what each already knew, that they were as well matched for one another, in life station, character, personality, and commitments, as much as two mature adults could reasonably expect. It was as if they had submitted profiles to a dating app and come up as a perfect match. Their challenge thus wasn't in disclosing background, coming to terms, resolving differences, confirming compatibility, or any of the other several things that dating must usually accomplish.

Their challenge wasn't even in deciding whether they were interested in attempting a new relationship after their prior marriages had each ended, in different ways. Moore knew he was lonely, missing a wife as a properly contesting, caring, and completing companion. Helena likewise knew she had capacities, ministries, and destinies that only a proper husband could fulfill.

That the two would be better together than apart had been clear from their first meeting. Helena and Moore were experiencing what every committed couple comes to know. The wife is only the left hand of life, material and fruitful but chaotic and decomposed, while the husband is only the right hand of life, patterned and reasoned but so rigid as to be incapable of bringing forth life. Paradise isn't heaven alone but a mix of sustenance and breath, of both feminine material and masculine meaning.

Moore and Helena might have admitted greater concern than they did for trying second marriages. They of course each had reservations about doing so, Moore not to taint a prior treasured marriage that ended far too soon with his wife's death, and Helena not to struggle and fail a second time for whatever reason. Yet their attraction to one another was sufficiently strong that they each suppressed those reservations.

What Moore and Helena may have suspected, or even come to know deep within each of them, is that every long-term marriage involves coming together again later in life. Life changes, sometimes suddenly, always dramatically, for both men and women over time. The person you marry isn't the person you bury or leave behind on your own way to glory. Each day brings a new adventure with a spouse who is newer and more different than older and the same.

Circumstances had deprived Moore and Helena of experiencing new chapters with their old spouses. Through prayer, reflection, and more than a little advice from others who knew them well, each of them grew in confidence that they should not let circumstances deprive them of experiencing new chapters with a new spouse.

And so, the challenge that Moore and Helena discerned wasn't *whether* to advance their relationship. Their challenge was instead *how* to do so. They needed a bridge from their separate pasts to the common future. And gradually, with the help again of Moore's elderly couple friends, they had discerned that another Holy Lands tour might just do the trick. Moore led Holy Lands tours usually

4

at least twice a year. Why not offer Helena a supporting role in the next trip?

Moore had an opportunity to lead a mixed group of high school, college-age, and graduate students on a Holy Lands tour. The high school students were from a private Christian school Moore had long supported. The undergraduate and graduate students were from the Christian university Moore had long ago attended, where he had maintained close professional relationships, especially with the university president. They would once again stay in the dormitories at Jerusalem University College.

Leading an Israel trip of youths and young adults might not be the perfect choice for Helena and Moore to take, test, and try a next step in their relationship. But Moore needed a female chaperone along on the trip. And who better than Helena?

Helena had gladly accepted Moore's offer for a second Holy Lands trip. Helena had barely been able to afford her first trip to the Holy Lands. She had committed to that trip to restore her relationship with her daughter Eva and give Eva a fresh direction in her life.

Helena's investment in her first Holy Lands trip had worked, far better than she had imagined possible. She just hadn't expected to receive Moore in the bargain. And she hadn't imagined getting to take a second trip to the Holy Lands, especially as a chaperone, at someone else's expense. Yet the second trip just made too much sense. The second Holy Lands tour was also the only way she and Moore could discern to take a next step in their relationship, whatever that step would entail. Helena was entrusting the details to her mysterious Lord.

Moore, though, had a little more in mind than just another inspiring Holy Lands trip. He hoped that by the trip's end, he would have found the time, place, and manner to propose to Helena, if all things continued to point as God's will in that direction. Moore even had a time, place, and manner planned, with an engagement ring in hand. Although they hadn't discussed it directly, Moore had the sense that Helena would welcome it and perhaps even expect it.

Moore settled into a seat beside Helena at the airport terminal gate to await the arrival of their twenty tour students and the departure of their flight to Istanbul and then on to Tel Aviv. The students, with the help of their parents or friends, were responsible for getting to the airport, through security and to the airport gate. Moore and Helena would be responsible for bringing them back. Moore and Helena had arrived at the airport gate extra early to welcome the first arrivers.

Though neither admitted it, Helena and Moore had the same thoughts while sitting beside one another to await the first student's arrival. *So, this is what it's like.* Helena soon turned to Moore with a small smile. Moore smiled back. Helena reached across to pat Moore's hand, bringing a bigger smile from Moore.

"Moore!" an elderly man's voice interrupted their brief reverie.

The elderly man had his elderly wife in tow, leading her by the hand up to where Moore and Helena sat. Moore jumped up to greet them both with warm hugs. Helena joined him.

"Are you ready for this?" Moore asked the elderly couple with a small smile and shake of his head.

"Probably not," the elderly man replied with a laugh, for which his wife gave him a poke in the side.

"Of course we're ready," she corrected her husband, "And we're entirely up to it, have no doubt."

The elderly woman gave her husband a stern look to be sure he agreed. He gave a sheepish shrug but nodded.

"Remember that your roles are simply wisdom, eyes, and discernment," Moore reminded the elderly couple, "While Helena and I handle the rest."

"As long as you two promise to get along," the elderly woman teased Moore and Helena, taking each by the hand and drawing nods and smiles from both.

Moore moved his carry-on bag from his seat so that the elderly man, his wife, and Helena could sit side by side. The elderly couple and Helena took their seats, while Moore stood waiting for the first students to arrive.

Moore soon began to greet the arriving students, one by one and in some cases two by two. He had already learned their faces, names, and backgrounds from applications they had submitted for the tour. He was pleased to get every one of them right. With each greeting, Moore would turn to Helena and the elderly couple to introduce them, too. And with each greeting, Moore would ask whether they were excited for the trip.

Moore hoped that each student appreciated that these moments before disembarking for a Holy Lands tour are extraordinary. Anyone who makes such a pilgrimage knows that they are preparing to witness afresh the incredible scandal that was the Son of God coming into the world.

Traveling to Israel is to have the land and its historical events force one to admit that God took human form in the one whom we know as Jesus Christ. A proper Holy Lands trip proves the materiality, time, and place of the image, model, and Savior of humankind on whom we are to look. Moore held high hopes that every student taking part in the trip would return transformed, holding their faith with a fresh, new, strengthened, and deepened grip.

The world Jesus entered became a different world because of the terms on which he left and manner in which he left. One leaves the old dead world and enters new eternal life when accepting those terms and acknowledging that manner. A proper Holy Lands trip should make all the more real and material those very terms, confirming one's rescue from the old dead world.

That transformation was the way in which Moore had come to understand Christ's strange parable of the shrewd manager, whom Christ lauded for cutting the debts owed his master before the master fired the manager. The manager's old role was ending. He must send his old world's wealth ahead into his new world, where he would benefit from having new friends.

When one world ends, it must cede its wealth to the new world that emerges. We can only store up treasure in heaven, sending that treasure ahead into our new world. The boundary woman Rahab hung her scarlet thread from the wall, pouring her old wealth into the new Israel that would arise out of her faith.

The happy tourist who steps onto the plane for the Holy Lands leaves an old dead world behind for a new world of eternal life. The traveler casts the dying wealth of the old world forward into new relationships in the promised land of eternal life.

As more students arrived, Helena began to collect the young women around her. They chatted animatedly in small groups. Instantly, Helena sensed not only their excitement but also their apprehension. Several had never been out of the country. None had been to the Middle East. Helena could see that her role on the trip might include not just protector and accountability partner but also comforter. The youth and immaturity of the young women surprised Helena, whose own daughter Eva, only slightly older, would have seemed significantly more poised and wiser.

The young men, of which the trip hosted an approximately equal number, gathered around Moore. They, too, were excited, although being young men, they took more care not to show it. On the whole, they exhibited less apprehension than the young women, but that reserve, too, may have been more feigned than true.

Moore watched as the activity around the gate door and attendant's desk heightened. The airliner had been at the gate when Helena and Moore had arrived much earlier, perhaps even overnight.

Seeing that they would board soon, Moore pulled his student list from his pocket. He already knew that all the students had arrived. He had kept a mental checklist. But just to be sure, he went down the list one by one to ensure that all students were present, while confirming that each had their boarding pass.

"Good to go?" Helena asked Moore brightly.

"All accounted for," Moore confirmed.

"Prayer?" Helena asked.

"Good idea," Moore agreed, adding, "You take the women, and I'll lead the men."

Helena smiled her appreciation at Moore's confidence in her, although she hadn't felt that confident in herself. Each of them gathered their students around them for a brief quiet prayer.

Within minutes, boarding had begun. Moore had booked Helena's flight with his own flight. In doing so, he had secured their seats together. But watching the young women huddled around Helena and how Helena engaged and supported each of them, Moore prepared for a change in seating plans. And sure enough, that request came barely a moment later.

"Mind if I swap seats?" Helena asked Moore, explaining that one of the young men had drawn a seat between two of the young women.

"Sure, go ahead," Moore smiled, shrugged, and nodded, being sure that Helena noticed his tinge of regret.

"You and I will have plenty of time together," Helena replied with a smile and light touch on Moore's arm, showing that she noticed and appreciated his regret.

They were soon aboard and settled in their seats. With further seat swaps, Moore sat alongside and around several of the young men, while Helena managed to gather more of the young women around her. The elderly couple had also done what they could to ensure that every member of the group felt cared for and included. Indeed, Helena could see that the elderly woman was already plying the young woman student beside her with questions and advice, in much the same way that the elderly woman had done for Helena's daughter Eva on their prior Holy Lands tour.

As Helena and Moore watched the students settle in around them for the long overseas flight to Istanbul, they each thought that they might just have a special trip to enjoy with the students. While they wanted every student to experience the trip as more than they could have imagined, Moore and Helena had their own special expectations for the trip, involving one another. Indeed, Moore hoped to have an unforgettable surprise for Helena late in the trip. And he had another surprise awaiting her in Istanbul.

2

"Mom!" a familiar voice called to Helena at the gate for the Tel Aviv flight in Istanbul's new airport.

Moore's trips to and from Israel typically went through one of three layover routes, either London, Frankfurt, or Istanbul. Moore had no favorite route. Each route had its own features to recommend it, London for the convenience of the English language and culture, Frankfurt for the typical German efficiency, and Istanbul for the distinct culture and remarkable history.

Istanbul airport is easily among the ten largest airports in the world by passenger volume. The new airport, combining the two older airports that until recently served the world region, has the largest single terminal building in the world, just barely larger than the equally spectacular new airport in Dubai. Moore liked Istanbul's old Ataturk Airport for its relative antiquity and its location hemmed in within the old city and seacoast. He liked Istanbul's new international airport for its convenience, cleanliness, and amenities.

Moore had paused his Holy Lands tour party at an attractive airport food court, en route from their arrival gate to the gate for the flight to Tel Aviv. Of course, the students needed food and refreshment after the long flight from Chicago. They also needed to choose new partners and form new groups within which to socialize. A couple of young women also needed some distance from the elderly woman who had shared generously with them her unbidden advice.

But Moore had another reason for gathering the students at Istanbul airport's food court. He wanted to remind them of the remarkable role the ancient city in which they had landed had played in Christianity's spread and development.

Constantinople was the seat of the reunited Eastern and Western Roman Empires from 324 A.D. until the Western Empire's fifth-century fall. Originally a Greek colony known as Byzantium, it briefly took the name *New Rome* until renamed in 330 A.D. after the Roman emperor Constantine the Great who had reunited the two empires. After the fifth-century fall of the Western Roman Empire, the Eastern Empire, or Byzantine Empire, continued for another thousand years. The Byzantine Empire dwindled badly toward the end of that long period, especially in the face of Ottoman conquests. Constantinople even suffered a fifty-plus year period of Crusader rule. Yet Constantinople largely continued as the Byzantine Empire's seat until an Ottoman siege finally toppled the city in 1453 A.D.

Despite its fall to the Ottomans, Constantinople remained a distinct and important historical enclave for the next 500 years, reflected in its spectacular architecture. The Hagia Sophia, the cathedral of the Eastern Orthodox Church, remains the city's crown jewel, rivaled by the Imperial Palace where Roman emperors lived, the Hippodrome, and the Golden Gate of the city's massive walls. Constantinople finally took the name *Istanbul* in 1930 after the Turkish War of Independence moved the new nation's capital to Ankara.

Despite what Westerners might think of it from its ancient history, Istanbul is no backwater. Today, Istanbul is Europe's largest city and the financial center of Turkey. Lying on a land bridge between Europe and Asia, Istanbul remains a strategic military, commercial, and cultural site.

Moore briefly reminded the students of the city's historic significance. But he took greater pains to point out to the student's the city's significance to the Christian faith. Constantine the Great, Constantinople's first Roman emperor, was the Roman Empire's first Christian emperor. Historian Eusebius records that on his way to battle to conquer Rome, Constantine and his troops saw a cross of light in the sky above the sun, with the words *you shall conquer*. A dream reinforced his vision. After his prophesied victory, Constantine ended Rome's persecution of Christians, legalizing the faith along with other religions and cults. Constantine later converted to Christianity and made it the empire's state religion.

The students would soon see that several Holy Lands sites, Christ's traditional Bethlehem birthplace prominent among them, bear the protective mark of Constantine the Great. Following his vision and victory, Constantine sent his mother Helena to Jerusalem and its environs to investigate and preserve Christian relics and sites. Constantinople's Hagia Sophia or other local sites would soon claim to hold Christ's crown of thorns, a piece of his tunic and girdle, drops of his blood, and pieces of the cross among those recovered relics.

Moore was well aware that his fellow traveler Helena bore the name of Constantine's famous mother, whose protective investigations the Holy Lands still mark. Moore knew, too, that the historic Helena was a divorcee, like his precious new friend.

The historic Helena's relationship with Constantine the Great's father was complicated, to say the least. Some historians call her his wife, while others assign her a lesser status. She was more of a commoner than one considered worthy of marrying a Roman military leader like Constantine's father. He would later divorce her to marry the daughter of a prominent Roman leader. Helena hid away with her son Constantine until her former husband's death, by which time Constantine had made his own friends among key Roman leaders. Remarkably, Helena rose to far greater prominence than she had ever held as a wife, after her son Constantine's great victory.

Moore had not missed these curious parallels, that he would meet and potentially wed his own Helena, in peculiar relationship to the Holy Lands.

The instant Helena heard her daughter's call, she jumped from her seat at the gate, looking for the call's direction, as a mother would naturally do, no matter the place or the hour of the day or night. Eva rushed to hug her mother in an excited embrace.

Moore watched mother and daughter embrace from a short distance away, smiling. Still hugging Eva, Helena caught Moore's mischievous smile, instantly realizing that he had been in on the surprise. Helena smiled back at

Moore in appreciation for the wonderful surprise. She hadn't expected to see Eva again for months.

"Mom," Eva said as they slowly released one another from their embrace, "Meet my friend René."

Helena was still reeling from her daughter's surprise appearance in Istanbul, when Eva revealed her own surprise. Eva had brought a male friend along.

Helena looked blankly at René, in the moment not knowing what else to do. René smiled warmly back at Helena. As Helena relinquished her grip on her daughter, she slowly turned to offer René first a hand and then a courteous return smile. René took Helena's offered hand formally and lightly, giving a small bow of respect and causing Helena's smile to grow in amusement.

Still not knowing what to make of the introduction, though, Helena shot Eva a glance that Eva properly read as a polite but firm request for an explanation.

"We work together, and he wanted to come along," Eva said more off-handedly than made sense in the circumstances.

Helena nodded in acknowledgment of Eva's curious statement, still not knowing what to make of the young man's presence alongside Eva or what to make of Eva's introduction. Yet Helena also knew that time would tell and that until then, she needed to be patient, although a hard thing for mothers to do on the subject of their daughter's relationships. Helena also considered in the moment that Eva herself might not entirely know of the grounds and motivations for the young man's presence.

Helena soon learned from polite conversation at the gate that René indeed worked with Eva. Helena took that disclosure to mean that René worked at the same national security agency office in New York where Eva had taken a job as an intelligence officer not long after her Holy Lands trip. Both Eva and René exhibited the reluctance to name the employer or job that Helena had come to expect. Intelligence officials don't generally advertise their activities.

Moore joined the three of them, saying to Helena in jest, "I hope you don't mind my inviting Eva. We figured she and René might make suitable additional chaperones for our many charges."

Helena feigned a punch at Moore's shoulder in mock protest, saying with a big smile, "So, you've been up to no good again. But I think we can make do with the arrangements."

Helena gave Eva a hug again, just as the gate attendant called for pre-boarding. The call spurred Moore into his usual action, checking that all students were present, accounted for, and ready for boarding. Several students swapped seats for fresh companionship. Moore urged Eva to take his seat beside Helena, leaving Moore to sit with René on the Tel Aviv flight.

On the flight from Istanbul to Tel Aviv, Helena mused more deeply over her daughter's decision to accompany her, with a male friend from her intelligence agency, on another Holy Lands trip. Helena needed to speak with Moore, who she suspected knew more of the cause. She couldn't imagine that Eva and René would make the trip without some ulterior purpose. And Helena could imagine several such other purposes, beyond getting to see more of the Holy Lands. She hoped Moore knew.

Meanwhile, a few rows back, Moore was getting to know René. Moore learned that the young man's cosmopolitan parents had named him after the French philosopher René Descartes. The young man did not elaborate on the meaning or import of his name. But Moore knew that René means *renewal* or *rebirth*.

Considering the young man seated comfortably beside him, Moore naturally wondered whether René had received the eternal Lord's rebirth. Responsible pastors tend to think that way, given that sharing the good news is their presumed calling. If Moore had met the young man by happenstance, just for this one flight, Moore probably would have asked the young man about his rebirth. But Moore instead figured that he would have the rest of the trip to learn. He also figured that the whole trip would involve sharing the good news of rebirth.

A few rows ahead, Eva was filling Helena in on the excitement of her new work in New York, once again in the indirect and highly limited manner that intelligence officers would find themselves permitted to disclose. Mother and daughter had stayed in long-distance touch. Helena had the broadest outline of the opportunities Eva had grasped and challenges she had faced. For Eva to share her excitement in person during the flight was a rich reward for Helena.

Yet inevitably, their conversation eventually turned to the young man sitting beside Moore a few rows back.

"So," Helena ventured slyly, in much the same manner Eva had teased Helena about Moore on their prior flight to Tel Aviv, for their first Holy Lands trip, "What's up with the young man?"

"I told you, he just wanted to come along for the trip," Eva replied with a shrug, more to amuse her mother than with any irritation.

Helena scowled at Eva, drawing a laugh.

"Okay," Eva resumed, "We're good friends. I mean, we decided we wanted to spend some time together outside of work. Moore's invitation came at the perfect time."

Helena nodded, waiting to see if Eva shared more. When she didn't, Helena prodded, "What do you think of him?"

Eva looked thoughtfully at her mother, letting Helena know she was indeed thinking deeply, more deeply than her mother might have expected. After a long pause, Eva answered, "He's brilliant but naive."

Helena raised her eyebrows in surprise, saying, "Naive is the last thing I'd assume about someone in that line of work."

Eva shook her head, replying, "It's funny, but while everyone's brilliant, everyone also seems strangely uninformed about things you'd assume everyday Americans would know. At least, Americans like us."

Helena raised her eyebrows in surprise once again. Eva soon explained. Turning to Helena to look her in the eyes, Eva said, "Mom, I don't think he knows anything about the Lord."

Eva's statement floored Helena. Helena had never regarded her daughter as someone especially concerned with that question, surely not when choosing her friends. Helena knew that their prior Holy Lands trip had impacted Eva's faith. Yet Eva had taken an intelligence agency job in New York not long after their return, which didn't seem to Helena like a new commitment to faith.

Lost in her own reaction, Helena realized that Eva was still looking at her, apparently awaiting Helena's response.

"Does that matter to you?" Helena asked gently, trying to ensure that her tone showed complete respect for Eva's expressed concern.

Eva looked down at her hands. Helena noticed Eva rubbing and regarding the empty ring finger of her left hand. Soon, Eva looked up again, into Helena's eyes.

"I think so," Eva replied.

Helena's eyes instantly grew moist with tears. She took a deep breath, reached over to place a hand atop Eva's hands, and answered, "Then this trip may be just the thing the two of you need."

Eva nodded, her own eyes moist with tears.

Helena's judgment about her daughter was exactly right in one sense. Although Helena had always been a church goer, Eva hadn't expressed her mother's interest in forms of faith. Eva was instead an inquirer, seemingly curious about everything except about traditional forms and rituals of faith.

Yet the prior Holy Lands trip had opened Eva's inner eye to the incredibly rich and detailed context, and entirely real and material circumstances, for the Christian faith. Encounters with the whispers, patterns, movements, and desires of the Spirit of Christ had simultaneously opened Eva's heart.

Eva had continued her new exploration of faith on her return from the Holy Lands. She didn't join a Bible study or begin regular attendance at a church. Eva instead continued along her own inquirer's path. But for the first time in her life, she could see that her path was indeed one of faith in the organizing principle and authoring life of Jesus Christ.

Unknown to Helena, Moore had helped Eva along that path. Eva had reached out to Moore on several occasions after their return from the Holy Lands, usually with thoughtful emails but a couple of times for telephone conversations. Eva's thoughtfulness impressed Moore. He also found that he could at times confirm or guide Eva along her inquirer's path.

One example was when Eva asked Moore about religious rituals, which Eva admitted she found off putting. Moore had replied that we all follow rituals continuously, in everything from greeting one another to eating, bathing, or going to bed. Religious rituals, Moore explained, seek to invoke and imitate the world's deeper cosmology, resting on Christ.

Although moderns think them weird or ridiculous, religious rituals simply reflect a more thoughtful and profound effort to align oneself with the world's deepest structures. Religious rituals address the metaphysical, not the physical, when the metaphysical guides and determines the purpose of one's life. Eva promptly understood and soon accepted Moore's proposition on rituals.

In a follow-up communication, Moore had helped Eva see that everything has a purpose and identity that one could call religious or metaphysical. A stool has its identity and purpose as a seat, which is a very fine and good use. A spoon has its identity and purpose for stirring and eating, both likewise wholly good and encouraging uses. Birds have purposes, and so do trees and streets and sunsets. And humans have the highest purpose, to represent the God who made all things after his own goodness.

Eva also had questions about religious judgments, especially the judgment of Christ. Moore suggested to Eva that everything judges by its purpose and identity. A spoon will instantly tell you whether you have used it properly or not. Yet so, too, will a bird, in its own way. A street will do likewise, especially when one departs from its straight or winding way. We also tell one another whether we use one another well and properly or not. Judgment is implicit and unavoidable in identity and purpose. Everything and everyone judges, continuously.

Moore shared with Eva that Christ simply judges as the ultimate pattern. The Son judges implicitly whether you meet his ideal or not. Judgment comes of its own accord. Yet the Son's ideal isn't simply to live and do as he did and instructed, as none of us entirely could. The Son's ideal, while fully warranting imitation, is instead primarily for us to acknowledge that he lived the perfect ideal, died the sacrificial death, and rose in resurrected life to give us the life we could not have without him.

Eva understood these tenets of the faith, that all come freely because of the price Christ paid. Yet Eva admitted to Moore that she lived and worked in a milieu that gave no attention to Christ's sacred ideal. Moore agreed with Eva that attention is the one thing we most have.

Neuropsychologists posit that while literally a million stimuli bombard our sophisticated senses, we consider only one at a time. Cold? Hungry? Want to listen to music? Yes, we process just one stimulus at a time. Yet we have some degree of choice over the extraordinarily few stimuli to which we attend. We choose whether to watch another television special or go to bed for school or work in the morning.

Moore and Eva agreed that an environment like New York, like virtually any other U.S. city of any size, is extraordinarily rich in stimuli designed to catch, captivate, hold, increase, and commit the attention.

They also agreed that in our consumer-driven, attention-grabbing, modern environments, attending the sacred requires unusual devotion. Paying attention to the sacred requires active receptivity to the metaphysical and divine. One must care more deeply about the highest ideals behind our senses than to the things that compete so continuously and effectively to grab them.

In the end, Eva came to the conclusion that attention is a moral act, changing both her and the things to which she gave her attention. Eva further concluded that to pay attention to another, whether the Son of God or a certain friend named René, is an act of generosity, indeed an act of love. Love attends to the other in pure regard for their

21

welfare. She knew she wanted René to know the moral grounds for attention, including the highest ideal and salvation of the Son of God.

3

The airliner touched down at Ben Gurion International Airport with its usual small bounce, giving the students aboard an extra bounce of excitement at having reached the Holy Lands.

Pilgrimage is a concept both foreign and familiar to Christians. The faith does not demand travel to the Holy Lands. One's faith in Christ is secure whether one makes the trip to Israel or not. But the faith certainly invites travel to the Holy Lands and associated sites. And Christian faith requires a certain kind of journey, spiritual if not literal, a figurative journey that literal travel to the Holy Lands can extravagantly spur.

The Christian's pilgrimage is a journey toward God. A follower of Christ does not pursue him to any other destination. A Christian's pilgrimage is into the heart of Christ. Christ is, after all, the pursuer. Our pilgrimage is not in that sense even one of travel or pursuit. Our journey is more like one of relinquishment, giving ourselves up to the Father's heart. A Christian's pilgrimage is thus to any place one hopes to encounter God.

Moore emerged from the sky bridge tunnel glad to see the students gathering in the terminal hall. A tour party's first gathering on Israel's soil always brought Moore special satisfaction and excitement. He felt not just called but born to share the history, reality, and inspiration of the Holy Lands, as if he, like one of those ancient shepherds in the hills outside Bethlehem, had witnessed the glory of Christ. Such is the depth of faith and passion in those who grow close to the Lord.

Moore soon had the group, both students and chaperones, moving smartly toward the baggage area, where Helena confirmed the shuttle bus. While the group awaited the delivery of their bags, Moore reminded the students of Israel's founding, focusing on its heralded first leader.

Ben Gurion International Airport, located outside Tel Aviv adjacent to the suburb of Lod, is Israel's largest airport. Since 1973, it has borne the name of Israel's primary founder and first prime minister David Ben-Gurion, who died in that year.

Ben-Gurion was a remarkable figure, properly revered in Israel and, by many, worldwide. He led the Jewish Agency in Palestine from 1935 until Israel's 1948 founding as a modern nation. Ben-Gurion was the first to sign

Israel's Declaration of Independence, of which he was a drafter. He then organized the several Israeli militias into the Israel Defense Force (IDF) during the 1948 Arab-Israeli War, also known as the First Arab-Israeli War. The First Arab-Israeli War grew out of a civil war in the region, one that with Israel's founding devolved into a war of national states.

Following Israel's victory in what became its war of independence, Ben-Gurion led Israel as its prime minister and minister of defense from 1948 until 1963, except for a brief break in 1954-1955. He spent his last decade of life in retirement at a modest kibbutz in Israel's southern Negev desert.

Moore shared with the students that the Israel Defense Force captured the airport in which they stood, in that 1948 war for independence. One student asked about its current safety, to which Moore was able to reply that no bombings or rocket attacks had hit the airport since then, despite targeted attacks.

Nor have any hijackings occurred out of Ben Gurion International Airport, although in 1972 Palestinian terrorists forced an airliner departing from Vienna to reroute and land there. Israeli special forces, including later Israeli prime ministers Ehud Barak and Benjamin Netanyahu, stormed and retook the landed plane. Communist Japanese Red Army terrorists also sprayed machine-gun fire into the terminal that same month, killing two dozen while injuring many others.

Moore's introduction helped the students appreciate the region's geopolitical tensions, evidence of which they could already see in the airport's prominent security and would see again in the region's many checkpoints.

Baggage in hand, the tour party boarded the shuttle bus to head to Jerusalem University College. Moore addressed the students again, this time about Tel Aviv and its environs, while the party waited for baggage handlers to load the last items and for the driver to prepare for the bus to depart.

Tel Aviv is a relatively new city on an ancient site. Jaffa was the prominent ancient city at the location, first inhabited around 10,000 years ago and recognized as a city by 1,800 B.C. Ottoman conquerors formed a settlement at Tel Aviv as a sort of Jaffa suburb, millennia later. But it was not until around 1910 that Jewish settlers gave the settlement its current Tel Aviv name.

From the start, though, those settlers planned Tel Aviv as a major city for Jewish settlement. Tel Aviv soon outgrew and then gradually incorporated Jaffa. After Israel declared its 1948 independence at Tel Aviv, and then prevailed in the First Arab-Israeli War, Tel Aviv formally annexed Jaffa.

Today, with a population just under a half million, Tel Aviv is Israel's largest city, if one doesn't count East Jerusalem as part of Jerusalem's total population. Otherwise, Tel Aviv is the nation's second-largest city behind the combined East and West Jerusalem. In either case, Tel Aviv is Israel's technological and commercial center, conveniently located along Israel's Mediterranean coastline and its sea-hugging land transportation route from Egypt north to Lebanon and Syria, and around to Iraq. Tel Aviv is also Israel's largest port.

Tel Aviv was briefly Israel's capital, from 1948 to 1950, before the nation afforded Jerusalem the historic and diplomatic honor. Yet given the sensitivity of Jerusalem as a political, religious, and historic site over which many make and hold claims, Tel Aviv continues to host 92 of the 97 embassies other nations have opened in Israel. The other five embassies relocated to Jerusalem only recently, when in 2018 the U.S. finally did so.

As the tour bus rolled out of the airport and on its way toward Jerusalem, the students could see a little of what makes Tel Aviv a cosmopolitan center, world-class tourist destination, and one of the world's most expensive places to live. The city attracts 2.5 million visitors each year to share with its young residents its exquisite beaches, beautiful parks, historic architecture, and exciting nightlife.

The tour bus soon completed its half-hour trip inland from the Mediterranean coast to reach its destination near Jerusalem University College, located within the historic Old City. The tour group members departed the bus to walk their bags the last short distance to the college. Check-in and a dormitory tour were mercifully brief. Within a short while, the party's members had retired to rest and recuperate from the trip and begin their adjustment to the seven-hour time difference.

Jerusalem University College's campus rests atop a quiet corner of the Old City, among other historic Christian organizations and nearby holy sites. The college's neighbors include the traditional Cenacle site of Christ's Last Supper and King David's tomb, the Dormition Abbey traditional site of Mary's death, and the city's Greek Orthodox seminary. The Anglican Bishop Gobat School built the college's original building in 1853 just outside the Old City's walls. It was among the first modern-era constructions, careful not to disturb Jerusalem's ancient city wall, New Testament times ritual immersion baths, and residences dating to the eighth and seventh centuries B.C., on and around the college's grounds.

Moore, too restless to retire in the dormitory, sat alone in the college's courtyard, overlooking the Temple Mount. The sun was already low in the western sky. Sensing a figure approaching from behind him, Moore turned.

"Join me?" Moore said to the approaching René, while motioning to one of the several empty seats alongside him.

René plopped himself into the seat toward which Moore had motioned.

"Beautiful, isn't it?" Moore asked, his gaze returning to the Temple Mount and Old City skyline.

René nodded.

"What do you know of the Temple Mount?" Moore asked René, with no clear idea of the young man's breadth or depth of scriptural or historical knowledge.

René shrugged, replying only, "Tell me."

Moore smiled, trying to read the young man's non-answer and blank expression. Finding no clue, Moore began.

"The golden dome you see is the Al-Aqsa Mosque, built atop the Temple Mount. It is among the world's largest mosques, able to accommodate around 400,000 Muslim worshipers."

Moore paused, again with a glance toward René to see if the young man gave any clue of his knowledge or interest. Again finding no clues in the young man's blank expression, Moore resumed.

"Size, though, isn't what makes Al-Aqsa significant to Muslims. They instead venerate the site as where their prophet Muhammad ascended on a winged horse. Of course, Muslims also recognize the Temple Mount as the location of the great Temple built by Israel's king Solomon, whom Muslims generally accept as among their prophets. Herod the Great completed the rebuilding of the Second Temple on the site, at around the time of Christ's earthly ministry. Mary and Joseph presented the infant Jesus at the Second Temple, where Christ also taught, and outside which he turned over the tables of the money changers."

Moore paused again to glance at the young man seated alongside him, looking for clues of recognition, especially about his references to the gospel accounts of Christ. Again, the young man showed no reaction.

Moore seldom spoke at length about the Muslim structures, sites, and history he and his tour parties encountered on their Holy Lands tours. Islam wasn't his expertise or interest. He knew enough to answer questions but generally took the view that the less he said, the better. In the case of the Temple Mount, though, Moore felt that he had to at least explain the nature of the structure that his party members saw on the sacred site.

"Is that the original dome?" René finally asked after a long pause.

"No," Moore answered, pleased at the young man's interest but disappointed at its subject. Moore had hoped that the young man would have a spiritual rather than material inquiry.

"The golden dome you see is one of several domes Muslims rebuilt on the site over the original Jewish temples, which Babylonian and Roman conquerors destroyed many centuries before Islam arose," Moore continued, adding, "Earthquakes and fires have destroyed several mosque domes and structures on the site. The dome you see is a concrete dome erected in the late 1960s and recovered with lead in the early 1970s."

Moore knew these and other details, although he had little interest in them. He didn't mind that his tone reflected his lack of interest. He'd much rather speak of spiritual, Christian, and even Jewish and Israeli matters, anything related to the Lord for whom he cared.

"Who controls access?" René asked, again with no particular clue regarding his level of interest or disinterest.

Moore felt another twinge of disappointment at the young man's choice of subjects but resolved again to answer as best he could, without hiding his own lack of interest in the subject. He wanted René to trust him as a source of reliable information and a willing partner in the young man's education.

"The Jordanian government administers the site," Moore answered, adding, "A Muslim cleric whom the Palestinians appoint controls religious activities on the site."

"Do we have access?" the young man asked.

"No, not presently," Moore replied, adding, "Muslim residents and visitors have access. Others haven't entered since the Second Intifada in 2000."

Moore was relieved to hear the approach of another individual from behind them, having grown tired of the conversation's direction and the opacity with which the young man conducted it. Moore turned to see Eva approach.

"Join us?" Moore said to her, smiling brightly while motioning toward another empty seat.

But René had already risen as if to go. Eva looked at René, then at Moore, and back to René, unwilling to resolve an apparent impasse.

"Let's take a walk," the young man proposed, ignoring Moore's invitation for Eva to sit with them.

Eva gave Moore an apologetic look.

"See you in a bit, I guess," she said to Moore, adding a small smile and shrug.

Moore smiled back, raising a forefinger to his brow to give Eva a tip of an imaginary cap. As Moore watched the two leave through the courtyard gate, he already felt a small bit of regret at having agreed to Eva's request to let the young man come along for the trip.

Moore had hardly settled back into his courtyard seat before he sensed another approach from the veranda behind him. Turning, Moore saw a welcome sight. Helena smiled at Moore as he rose quickly, motioning her toward the seat beside him that René had just vacated.

"Any sign of her?" Helena asked as she took her seat.

"You mean Eva?" Moore asked as he settled back into his own seat.

Helena nodded.

"She and René just left for a walk," Moore said. He looked toward the setting sun before adding, "They shouldn't be gone long. It'll soon be dark."

"Let's hope they have enough sense to be back before then," Helena replied with a small roll of her eyes, adding, "We sure don't need any drama like last time."

Moore chuckled, nodding, but replied with a smile, "Worked out okay, though, didn't it?"

"Yes," Helena replied, reaching for Moore's hand to give it a squeeze as she did so.

The two sat quietly together, looking over the Old City's glittering skyline. Neither wanted to speak. Each wanted the moment to last. If they could have stopped the sun at its low angle to let the evening linger, they each would have. Gradually, though, the evening began to turn to night.

Helena was the first to break the silence, asking, "Should we be worried?"

Moore shook his head before replying with a wry grin, "Not about these two. If two intelligence officers can't take care of themselves on an evening's stroll, then we've got bigger problems than we think."

Helena smiled at Moore's light jest. But Moore had given Helena the opening she needed for the question she had wanted to ask.

"They're not just here to help us out, are they?" she asked, refusing to hide her concern.

Moore shrugged but shook his head and answered, "No, they're not. That's as much or as little as I know."

"Any guesses?" Helena asked again.

"Well," Moore slowly surmised, "My only guess is that it might have something to do with Eva's prior contacts here. Why else would they send a new agent out here?"

Helena nodded, replying, "And René?"

"I can't figure him out," Moore replied, shaking his head. He turned to Helena, studying her emotional condition briefly before deciding to continue with, "He's a completely different person, of course, but the way he left with Eva reminded me of the Russian."

Helena winced. Noticing, Moore resumed, saying, "I know. Neither of us wants a reprise of the last trip. But René seems up to something he won't disclose, and I'm not sure Eva knows all of it."

Eva had indeed joined a mysterious Russian on unexplained jaunts amid their prior Holy Lands tour. The Russian had turned out to be a money launderer and probable arms and antiquities dealer. Eva's aid in exposing the Russian's dealings had led to his arrest. But the matter had also left some hard feelings between the Israeli national intelligence agency Mossad and the U.S. intelligence agency for which Eva subsequently went to work.

Moore and Helena sat again in silence, as night fell. Once again, Helena was the first to break the silence.

"You're right," Helena finally piped up, causing Moore to turn to her and tip his head in curiosity.

"She's going to be fine," Helena explained, adding, "And it's completely different this time."

Moore nodded, joining Helena in a warm smile. Helena paused before resuming, saying, "I only hope the trip helps René see what Eva wants him to see."

Helena looked into Moore's eyes, waiting to see if Moore recognized both Eva's concern and her interest.

Moore looked back, nodding while saying only, "Exactly."

Heartened once again at Moore's pastoral insight and passionate character, Helena reached over and gave his hand another warm squeeze.

"Time to retire," Helena said, rising from her seat.

"I'll walk you back to the dormitory," Moore offered.

"No," Helena replied with a sly smile, placing a hand on Moore's arm while adding, "Let's not get the students talking."

4

Unusually, Moore was not the first tour party member in the college cafeteria early the next morning. Two voices hailed him when he entered. He moved easily to their table to join them.

"Good night's sleep?" Moore asked the elderly couple in greeting, as he took a seat with them.

Each of them shook their heads, looking at one another while laughing and groaning.

"Went to bed too early," the elderly man explained, "And got up too early, too."

They both laughed again. The elderly woman gave her husband a poke in the ribs.

"Accommodations alright?" Moore asked.

Both nodded, the elderly woman saying quietly, "Very nice. The Gloria has more Old City charm, even if fewer of the conveniences that we wouldn't use in any case."

"We won't miss that it has no pool or gym," the elderly man rejoined, drawing chuckles.

The elderly couple seldom stayed in the college dormitories with Moore's tour groups, never in the summer because of the heat. The dormitories lack air conditioning. But even in the early spring, as for this trip, they often chose a nearby hotel over the dormitories. They had done so in this instance because of the group's energetic youth whose late-night antics might have kept them from a good night's sleep.

Jerusalem's Old City offers attractive, top-end accommodations, especially if the guest is willing to stay outside the Old City walls. The elderly couple usually stayed at the King David Hotel near the college. In this instance, though, the elderly couple was staying at the Gloria Hotel, just inside the Old City's Jaffa Gate.

"Did you do alright?" the elderly woman asked Moore.

Moore looked down at his hands before answering, "Turned in later than I should have."

"Anyone keep you up?" the elderly woman asked with a sly smile.

"Well, yes, in fact," Moore answered with a chuckle of recognition over his elderly friend's inference. He explained, "We had a nice time watching the skyline together as the sun set."

But Moore shook and lowered his head again, adding, "Eva and her young man left for an evening walk together and didn't come back until the middle of the night."

"Ooh," the elderly woman replied, shaking her own head, "That must have concerned Helena. Walking around the Old City in the middle of the night isn't an especially wise choice."

Moore nodded, replying, "It seemed a little too much like last time, which I'm not going to let happen again."

Students had been wandering quietly into the cafeteria, getting food or coffee from the sideboard, and sitting alone or in twos and threes to sip and eat. Moore looked up to see Helena enter, just as she stood in a spot of bright morning sunlight streaming through the cafeteria's large windows. The sight of her took Moore's breath away.

"She's beautiful, isn't she?" the elderly woman said quietly to Moore, placing a gentle hand on his forearm atop their small table.

Moore smiled and nodded, but he was already rising. Stopping to say good morning to students as he passed, Moore made his way to Helena.

"Sleep okay?" Moore asked.

Helena shook her head no.

"Me, either," Moore replied.

"Eva didn't get in until 3 a.m.," Helena said.

"René slipped in at the same time," Moore replied.

"Did you say anything to him?" Helena asked.

Moore shook his head, replying, "I pretended I was asleep. But we're having a good chat this morning."

"Looks like now's your chance," Helena replied, tipping her head toward a sleepy figure entering the cafeteria.

Seeing René surveying the room for Eva, Moore pointed Helena to where the elderly couple was seated, watching. Helena moved to join them. Moore headed for René.

"Grab some coffee and let's have a chat," Moore greeted René. Moore forced a smile that he didn't feel like sharing.

"That's alright," René replied coolly. Motioning toward a seat near the door, he added, "I'll just wait over here for Eva."

Feeling his anger rising but forcing calm, Moore shook his head slowly, saying simply, "We're talking. Can I get you some coffee?"

René looked back at Moore. Reading Moore's firm tone and serious expression, he nodded, saying, "Thanks. Black."

Moore pointed to a table to the side, away from where the others sat. The room was filling. Moore moved quickly to grab a cup of coffee and join René at the table to which Moore had pointed.

"What time did you turn in last night?" Moore asked in as kind a voice as he could manage, as he sat across from René at the small table.

"Oh, not late," René replied.

Moore raised his eyebrows, catching the young man's glance.

"Well before midnight, anyway," the young man added, looking straight at Moore.

Moore looked back at the young man, assessing. Seeing the same blank wall that the young man had already several times presented, and thinking of the young man's intelligence agency employment, Moore made an instant judgment to be blunter and franker than he would have with a different young man.

"That's not true," Moore replied in a quiet, matter-of-fact tone. Still looking calmly back at the young man, Moore tipped his head slightly while adding, "Indeed, that's a lie."

Moore watched the young man's face for a reaction but saw none. Instead, René shrugged. Still looking straight back at Moore, he replied, "You were asleep. And it doesn't matter."

Although his anger was again rising, Moore looked calmly back at the young man, saying only, "Telling the truth always matters. Those who lie soon fool only themselves. And I am responsible for everyone's safety, security, and moral welfare on this trip. I can't have you and Eva gallivanting around in the middle of the night, no matter what you are doing."

René continued looking straight back at Moore but now irritably. With almost a sneer, René replied, "I swear, I was in bed before midnight. And it's no big deal."

Moore looked away from the young man in disappointment, ending their stare down. But Moore wasn't finished.

Speaking just loud enough for the young man to hear but as if speaking to himself, while looking across the cafeteria to the sunlight streaming through the big windows, Moore mused, "A lie is a wrong, an offense against both oneself and the other. A lie also offends God. Christ admonished never even to swear an oath but to let a yes be yes and a no be no."

Moore paused to let his words sink deeply into the young man, although Moore continued looking away, out the cafeteria's big sunlit windows. Yet once again, Moore wasn't quite finished. He resumed, "Lying to another when you both know that you are lying is an even greater offense than an effective lie, one that the other believes to be the truth. Lying while expecting the other to accept what the other knows to be a lie attempts to make the other one's subordinate, one's stooge and lackey."

Moore rose slowly, stretching, smiling, and still looking out the cafeteria windows, aware that the students who had by then filled the cafeteria were probably watching him, expecting instructions. Finally turning to René while still smiling, Moore asked, "Can I get you some more coffee?"

The young man looked blankly back at Moore, too stunned to answer. Just then, Eva joined them.

"Hey," she asked brightly, "How's everyone?"

"Great," Moore answered, while the young man said nothing. Moore continued, "Late night for you two, huh?"

Eva looked from Moore to René and back to Moore. René began opening his mouth to reply, but Moore cut him off, turning to Eva to say, "Right around 3 a.m. is a late night, no matter which side of the world you're on."

Eva gave Moore a sheepish look, saying, "It turned into a longer walk than we expected."

Having won the honest acknowledgment that he expected from Eva, Moore turned to René, who still sat at his small table.

"You're off the trip," Moore told him quietly, just loud enough for both Eva and René to hear, adding, "You've got a room at the Gloria Hotel."

With that announcement, Moore turned to join Helena and the elderly couple at their table for a moment before commencing the morning's study.

"What just happened?" the stunned Eva asked, still standing at the young man's table.

René shrugged, "I told him we were in before midnight."

"What did he say?" Eva asked, already shaking her head in disappointment at the young man's answer.

"He said he didn't think lying was good for anyone," René answered matter of factly, adding, "And he said he had to protect his tour party."

Moore had returned to the center of the room, encouraging the students to finish breakfast and meet in five minutes in the adjacent college courtyard.

"Let's talk," Eva said sternly to René.

As she spoke, Eva tipped her head toward the door to the courtyard to indicate that René should follow. She then turned and walked off, leaving him sitting disconsolately alone at the table. The young man took a deep breath, rose slowly, and followed.

Once he had the students comfortably assembled in the courtyard, Moore began with his tradition of introductions, allowing each student to share their name and say a few words about their reason for joining the trip. While the high school students along for the trip all knew one another, they didn't know the college and graduate students.

Just as Moore planned, the students had a good time clapping, smiling, and laughing over one another's introductions. Moore called on each student by name, as he guided the introductions around the circle of students in the courtyard. As he did so, he noticed Eva and René off in the courtyard's corner in quiet discussion.

When the students had concluded their introductions, Moore reminded the students of the trip's itinerary, for which the students had spent weeks in preparatory studies.

"The college here in Jerusalem is our base camp," Moore began, explaining, "By beginning, returning, and ending here at the college, you'll have ample opportunity to explore Jerusalem's holy sites. Those explorations will begin late this morning."

"Yet as you know," Moore continued, "This trip will focus on the Galilee region in which Joseph and Mary raised Jesus and that Jesus made his ministry home. And so, we'll be making the two-hour-plus trip north to that region

40

tomorrow and will stay at locations there off and on, when not returning to the college."

Moore had indeed arranged a more-complex itinerary for this tour than for others he had led up and down Israel. Moore often lodged his parties solely or primarily at the college, both to save on overnight expenses and for the ease of administration. Yet because this trip focused on Christ's Galilee life and ministry, Moore had arranged several overnight lodgings in that northern Israel region, both to save on the travel time back and forth to the college and to ensure that the students got a good taste of local life.

Moore was also beginning this trip in a different fashion than most of his other Holy Lands tours, to accommodate his eager students. In the usual case, Moore wanted to get his tour party members into the field quickly to visit and explore the historical sites they had come so far to see. Moore typically avoided Jerusalem's several outstanding museums, including the Jerusalem Museum and Tower of David Museum, at least until nearer the end of the tour, when his guests might appreciate a recap of sorts.

But because the students would spend most of their time in the Galilee region, Moore wanted to expose the students to Jerusalem's treasures in an expedited manner. While he regretted missing extended visits to some of the traditional Jerusalem sites, Moore felt that a couple of Jerusalem museum visits might suffice to make up the difference.

"If you're all ready to begin," Moore continued his address to the waiting students, "Then we'll make our way to the National Campus for the Archaeology of Israel, where you'll see some of the treasures Israel's Antiquities Authority has acquired under the 1978 Law of Antiquities, authorizing the Authority to take possession of ancient artifacts. You'll also have some time to spend today at the

41

adjacent Israel Museum and Bible Lands Museum, right here in Jerusalem. Tomorrow, we'll be off to the Galilee region."

Moore concluded by inviting prayer from one of the graduate students whom Moore had already identified as a sound and inspired student leader.

Helena was at Moore's side when the prayer concluded, ready to help lead the group out the courtyard gate. Yet noticing two figures approaching from the courtyard's corner, Moore called out to the students, "Five minutes for a last snack, sip, or restroom break. Then meet at the courtyard gate."

René and Eva waited for the students to recede to the cafeteria before joining Moore and Helena.

"I have an apology to make," René said to Moore. Extending his hand for Moore to shake, René added, "I was wrong for not telling you the truth about last night."

Moore shook the young man's hand, while nodding and waiting to see if the young man had anything more to say. He did, the young man adding, "Would you permit me to rejoin the tour, on my assurance that you will not see a repeat of last night?"

Moore knew his answer. But he also sensed an opportunity.

"Would you please give us a minute?" Moore replied to the young man, while indicating that he wished to step aside to confer with Helena.

René, with Eva at his side, nodded respectfully. Helena looked questioningly at Moore as the two moved to the edge of the courtyard where René and Eva had just been conferring.

"Too much to explain right now," Moore said quietly to Helena, adding, "Other than that I told him he was off the tour for safety and security reasons, after he lied to me and refused to recant."

"So, what do you want to do?" Helena asked.

Moore smiled, saying, "I suspect you already know, but I wanted to hear what you think."

Helena smiled back but said nothing. So, Moore resumed, saying, "I'm not as concerned about Eva as I am about the others and about René himself. I'm pretty sure Eva can take care of herself. But we need to get through to René, not just for safety and security but also for other reasons."

Helena nodded, saying, "So, we're letting him come along?"

"For now," Moore replied, asking, "Are you sure you're alright with that?"

Helena nodded.

"Then let's be sure he understands the terms," Moore continued, while motioning gently for Helena to lead them back to the waiting young couple.

Rejoining Eva and René, Moore put a hand on the young man's shoulder, saying, "Thank you for the sensitivity. You're welcome to join us as long as Helena and I can depend on your reliability and veracity, just as is true for every other member of our tour party."

Moore gave the young man's shoulder a squeeze, while encouraging him, "Now you'd better get this young woman a quick snack and refreshment before we begin our morning's tour."

Moore naturally reflected on the young man's actions and motivations at moments throughout the rest of the day. Moore confirmed in his reflections that his revulsion to the young man's lies and, moreover, to the young man's willingness to manipulate Moore with those lies, wasn't simply a moral issue. The young man's lies and deceptions didn't simply offend Moore.

Rather, Moore's concern was with the door that opened wide to the evil that would soon possess the liar.

Moore knew that we all lie. Moore admitted that he had done so on far too many occasions, much to his shame and, even more shamefully, to the loss and injury of others. Moore had gradually learned the harmfulness of lies to the liar and to the lied. He had also gradually learned to recognize and repent of his own lying. Moore had learned to hate his own lies enough to stop them, both to stop the harm the lies did to others and the harm the lies did to Moore himself.

Moore watched the young man escort Eva around the National Archaeology Campus and two museums later that day. He hoped to have the opportunity to share his reflection with René, to let the young man know that Moore wasn't just imposing an old-fashioned, rigid morality for the sake of conformity.

Moore wanted the young man to understand that the evil that lying invites into one's soul destroys its host. Many things possess us, using us for their ends. Governments, employers, charities, churches, and causes, and certainly also family members, neighbors, and friends, turn us to their better or worse ends. So, too, do ideologies, philosophies, and faiths, sometimes for better ends, while other times for worse ends. But evil is unique in seeking to destroy the one whom it employs.

Moore suspected, from his conversations with René and intimations from Eva, that René had no sense of the hidden realm within which principles, patterns, agencies, and entities operate to influence us. The young man appeared to be a secularist, a materialist, one who thought little if anything of their even being a divine, supernatural, or spiritual realm, even though the young man so clearly operated under the influence of that hidden realm. René was, after all, an intelligence officer, given to detecting and deploying hidden systems, which in themselves fall so easily under the influence of hidden entities and agencies.

Moore thus wanted the Holy Lands tour to awaken René to the hidden realm in which he operated, under the influence of which he acted, and which he needed to learn to recognize in order to properly align himself with that realm's ultimate good. Moore wanted the young man to come to know the singular power and purpose of the Son of God within and over that hidden realm.

Little did Moore know that the young man would soon have encounters that would leave no doubt of the reality of the scriptures' divine realm.

5

Helena watched Moore eagerly point out to the students the fascinating exhibits of the National Campus for the Archaeology of Israel. Helena could see that Moore was entirely in his element when sharing with the students his passion for the story and lands of Israel.

Helena discerned that she didn't mind Moore's passion. Although she knew she sought Moore's attention, she found that she had no jealousy for the ardor Moore exhibited to the students, over what others might have regarded as inconsequential artifacts that the National Campus exhibited.

Helena was instead glad, indeed deeply appreciative, of Moore's interest. She respected Moore's Holy Lands passion not because he was a know-it-all, not because he was a nerd interested in facts more than people. Moore was neither. Helena respected Moore's passion for Israel because of his deeper passion for the Lord who chose it as his earthly home.

The Israel Antiquities Authority stores and preserves, at the National Campus and other sites, hundreds of thousands of Holy Lands artifacts, from prehistoric times through biblical times right into the Ottoman Empire's rule of the region. Those artifacts most notably include the Dead Sea Scrolls, generally regarded as the Twentieth Century's greatest archaeological find. The Antiquities Authority employs several experts full time, simply to clean, preserve, and document scroll fragments, and make images available to others for study.

The National Campus exhibits, though, include much more evocative items of ancient times than tiny parchment scraps of Dead Sea Scrolls. Second-century Roman swords and javelin, only recently discovered hidden behind stalactites deep in an Ein Gedi cave, are an example. Jews rebelling from their Roman occupiers had doubtless hidden those tools of war in their desert hideaway, after recovering them from the battlefield.

Other National Campus displays include biblical-era coins, pottery, and beams, lintels, cornices, capitals, and other architectural elements. The coins include not just Roman, Greek, and Persian gold and silver items exchanged in the Holy Lands but also items that the Jews minted in commemoration of their kings and high priests. One stash, discovered in 1975 in excavations at the southern wall of the Temple Mount, includes coins that rebel Jews minted in 69 A.D. during the Jewish War just before the Temple's 70 A.D. destruction.

Ancient mosaic floors and inscribed walls, translated for their historical content, bring the National Campus displays to further life. While archaeologists excavated many of the items in Jerusalem, the Antiquities Authority also brought items to the National Campus from Galilee, Caesarea, Tiberias, the Golan Heights, the Judean foothills to Jerusalem's west, and Samaria.

Eva and René meandered among the exhibits, chatting now and then with the students, throughout the day. They also now and then brought observations about, and inquiries from, the students back to Moore or Helena. One student was hungry, another thirsty, and another feeling a little nauseous, with which Helena helped. One pair of students had questions about the Temple's destruction, while another student had a question about excavating ancient sites, which Moore answered.

Both Moore and Helena thus felt satisfied and secure in their supervision of the students. Yet they also knew that they were only on secure museum grounds, not traveling about Israel and walking up and down busy city streets. They knew that their greater challenges were ahead of them.

Both Helena and Moore also found moments to watch Eva and René interact. Helena once pointed out to Moore how well they seemed to get along and relate. Eva tended to follow the young man wherever his interest took him, more than the young man followed Eva. But René seemed happy to investigate with Eva anything in which she expressed an interest, and the young man listened with interest to Eva when Eva had something to share.

Only one matter arose, around midafternoon, that gave Moore and Helena any pause for concern. Eva had come to Helena saying that René had gone to a restroom feeling lightheaded and had not yet come out. Helena sought Moore, whom Eva directed to the restroom. Inside, Moore found the young man leaning heavily against a washbasin, his head hanging down. Moore approached.

Assuming the young man had seen or heard Moore enter the restroom, Moore put a hand on the young man's shoulder to ask, "Sick to your stomach?"

René jumped at Moore's voice and touch, jerking his head up to regard Moore with a wild, entranced look.

Moore stepped back out of shock at the young man's appearance, saying, "Whoa! Whoa! Hold on there. It's just me."

But René composed himself almost as quickly as he had jumped at Moore's voice and touch.

Moore watched the wild look fade from the young man's eyes, saying, "I'm sorry. I didn't mean to startle you."

"No, no," René replied apologetically. Eager to reassure Moore, the young man explained, "I'm alright. I'll be fine in another moment. I just got a little lightheaded, maybe from the lack of sleep or something I ate. I probably just need some fresh air."

Moore nodded, letting his startled look of concern dissipate. He let the young man take a deep breath before following him out the restroom door. Moore gave Helena and Eva a thumbs-up sign as René headed slowly for an exit toward the sunshine outside. Eva joined him, while Moore returned to Helena's side.

"Just feeling the effects of the travel and lack of sleep, or maybe something he ate," Moore related to Helena, adding, "He says he'll be alright."

"You worried?" Helena asked Moore.

Moore paused before answering hesitantly, "Maybe a little."

"Shall we take him back to the college to get in bed or for medical care?" Helena asked.

"No, no," Moore replied quickly, "It's not that."

Helena tipped her head at Moore, giving him a look of curious concern. But Moore shook his head, unable to articulate what his intuition was hinting. Moore only knew that something hadn't been right about the look in the young man's eyes. Moore hadn't startled René. The young man had been seeing something.

By late afternoon, Moore had exhausted the students with his impassioned descriptions of the items they explored in the displays spread in and around the National Campus and its adjoining museums. Moore and Helena, with the help of Eva and a recovered René, gathered the students to head back to the college for dinner and discussion. The elderly couple, exhausted hours earlier, had already retired to their hotel.

Back at the college, most headed to their dormitory for a change of clothes or brief lay down, before drifting back to the cafeteria for pre-dinner conversation and refreshment. Helena, Eva, and René likewise retired for a respite.

Moore instead sat alone in the shade along the courtyard's edge, gazing at the bright Old City vista while considering the day's events. His thoughts soon returned to the young man's wild expression when Moore encountered him in the museum restroom. Moore's thoughts slowly turned to, of all things, demon possession.

On Holy Lands tours, Moore often had questions from tour party members about Christ's healing of so many demoniacs. The gospel's demon possession and exorcisms are obstacles to the faithful understanding of many. Moderns seeing the world through their lens of secular materialism don't generally credit the construct of demons and credit even less accounts of demon possession and exorcism.

Moore knew enough of the traditional thought and theological interpretations of those gospel accounts, to share interesting answers. But he wanted his answers to be helpful, not just interesting information. Moore had thus gradually found a way to turn the peculiar aspect of the demonic into an understandable psychology and phenomenology, he hoped, without giving up entirely on the ancient construct.

Sitting alone in the courtyard shade, Moore considered more deeply what he made of the young man's demonic demeanor in that instance when Moore had encountered him in the restroom. Moore believed the young man to be unfortunately far too open to demonic possession, if, as it appeared, he lacked Christianity's unifying and protective framework.

From multiple scriptural accounts, Moore believed God to be the author of both unity and multiplicity. God both gives his creation its organizing pattern and purpose, in grand and particular unity, while also dividing his creation into distinct, balancing categories.

God, for instance, made the earth for its purpose but divided its surface from its air and its land from its waters. God likewise made the animal kingdom but had humankind name the animals in their distinct categories. And God made humankind, while dividing humankind into male and female, and giving each individual distinct limbs, functions, roles, and capacities. Pentecost itself, that eternal and episodic connection between heaven and earth, between God's Spirit and humankind, involves the descent of a single Spirit spread into many languages through many flames.

Moore had seen many psychological issues in his pastoral counseling, everything from schizophrenia to multiple personalities, severely addictive behaviors, affective disorders, compulsions, depression, and delusion. He had also seen more than a few individuals whom he could just as well have regarded as being possessed of a demonic principle, pattern, or personality, whether of lust, greed, pride, power, or other psychopathy.

While he was certainly no psychologist, Moore had gradually come to believe that many of those conditions, if not all of them, included spiritual aspects, among their other psychological, mental, physical, biological, chemical, and other dimensions. Moore had discerned that God's creativity authors both multiplicity, multiple categories, multiple capacities, and multiple identities on the one hand, while also unifying and integrating that multiplicity into necessary, whole, ordered, and healthy unities. Moore had come to see that when God is absent or hidden, healthy multiplicity can fracture into chaos, even into the demoniac.

Moore thus considered that the young man René, without the secure mooring that a vital Christian faith would have provided, might be unfortunately subject to distorting and destructive principles, patterns, and personalities. Moore also considered that those distortions might be especially prevalent within and around the intelligence agency community. René, in short, might well be under attack by another intelligence agent or by the demonic deceptions that agents employ among and against one another.

The first students were returning to the cafeteria, interrupting Moore's thoughts. A few students joined Moore in the courtyard shade. Moore soon rose to ensure that the students took part in the cafeteria's dinner fare, so that they could have their evening's discussion. Helena and

Eva joined the students, sitting with René and saving a seat for Moore.

Moore moved from table to table, listening to the students share their thoughts about the day's explorations at the National Campus. Moore always tried to judge his audience's temperature before leading a discussion, whether the students might be tired, energized, eager, or already overwhelmed. As was often the case, Moore found a little of everything among the students. The first full day of a Holy Lands trip is often the hardest, when the party's members don't yet have a comforting and guiding routine to follow.

Moore joined Helena, Eva, and René for only a few minutes before jumping back up from their table to encourage the students to move to the courtyard. Moore could see that a few were learning toward returning to their dormitory beds, their inner clocks still confused by the travel.

"Nazareth is our destination tomorrow," Moore announced, once he had the students' attention in the courtyard. Moore added, "Nazareth is not, strictly speaking, a Sea of Galilee town, like Capernaum, Bethsaida, Chorazin, and even Tiberias. Nazareth is instead a Lower Galilee town, on a common approach to the Sea of Galilee."

The students sat in chairs and on steps in the shade along the courtyard perimeter, looking out over the Old City, while Moore stood in the courtyard's bright sunlight in front of them.

"We each tend to have a sentimental vision of Nazareth," Moore continued, introducing his theme for the excursion, "Especially those of us raised in the faith."

Seeing a few quizzical looks among the students, Moore explained, "Although Mary bore Jesus in their census home of Bethlehem, near us here in Jerusalem,

Nazareth was where Mary and Joseph lived as individuals younger than yourselves when betrothed. Nazareth was also where Mary received the angel's announcement that she would bear the Messiah Jesus and where Mary and Joseph returned with the boy Jesus after their refuge in Egypt. We thus tend to think of Nazareth as a quaint village where the young Jesus learned his father Joseph's carpentry trade."

Moore paused to ensure that the students saw his point. Seeing several students nod, Moore continued.

"The gospel account even tells us that Nathanael, who lived in the nearby but considerably more-affluent Cana, where Jesus turned water into wine, even asked the disciple Philip if anything good could come from Nazareth. Clearly, no one thought much of Nazareth. Remember that Nazareth was also where the townsfolk rejected and nearly murdered Jesus, even though he was one of them, raised among them from boyhood. God indisputably chose a relative backwater, a place about which few thought much, in which to raise his Son, in its abject humility much like the Bethlehem animal shelter in which Mary bore the Son."

Again, Moore paused to confirm the students' comprehension and interest, before resuming.

"But I want to challenge you to see Nazareth in another perspective, closer to what the village meant to the region and time. While Nazareth was a fairly small village, the surrounding hills of which kept it relatively sheltered, it still played significant regional roles in commerce and conflicts that stretched across the known world."

Moore continued on, less concerned now with the students' attention, more compelled by the story.

"Residents of Nazareth, likely including Mary's husband Joseph, who raised Jesus and taught him the carpentry trade, presumably walked the relatively short distance to work on Herod Antipas' fabulous constructions in nearby Sepphoris. We will view excavations of those structures. You may see stones that Joseph, among many other Jews, cut, moved, and placed in Sepphoris, perhaps even with the help of the young Jesus."

Sensing that he needed to move from his inadvertent lecture to student discussion, Moore moved quickly on.

"Pits, caves, and tunnels that residents of Nazareth dug deep into the limestone beneath their homes, even as much as three levels deep, show that the Nazarenes also hid their property from the taxation, and their women and children from the slaughter, abuse, theft, sale, and slavery, of Roman soldiers. Nazareth even played a hideaway role in the Jewish War that began in 66 A.D. and led to the Temple's 70 A.D. destruction."

Knowing that he had said enough to stimulate student discussion, Moore concluded, "In a way, understanding Nazareth helps one understand the full gospel account, from Genesis to Revelation. I hope you'll see Nazareth tomorrow as more than a quaint village in which Mary learned that she would bear and, with her carpenter husband Joseph, raise the Son of God."

Several students had already raised their hands with comments or questions. Moore called on a couple of them, each time asking another student or group of students what they thought of the comment or how they would answer the question. Moore wasn't interested in conducting a typical classroom format, where the teacher is the authority and the students consumers of information. Moore instead wanted his students thinking, questioning, answering, and exploring, even leading rather than simply following.

Moore loved his youth and young adult Holy Lands tours for that very reason, that he found the students willing or even eager to accept responsibility for their own learning. On some of his trips leading older adults, Moore had at times felt like they expected him to take an expert's stance and to lecture. The youth and young adults instead seemed to respect Moore without making him feel as if they needed him on a pedestal.

Moore soon brought the students' discussion to a close, not wanting to entirely tire them out on the tour's first full day. He could tell that he had already lost several students to regenerative daydreaming. With a brief prayer of thanks and for a good night's rest, Moore sent the students on their way to the cafeteria for evening snacks and refreshments, maybe a few games or some lingering conversation, and then on to their dormitories for the night.

Eva and René spent only a few minutes chatting and snacking in the cafeteria before each retiring for the night. Helena lingered with Moore.

"Satisfied with the day, Captain?" Helena teased Moore.

"Mostly," Moore nodded with a wan and tired smile.

"Still concerned about our study subject, huh?" Helena asked, guessing over Moore's hesitation about the day.

"You mean René?" Moore replied, to which Helena nodded.

Moore thought for a moment longer before replying, "Yes, but I'm also realizing that on this trip, he's in God's hands much more than mine."

6

Moore was in the cafeteria early in the morning, ready to take the students north on the two-hour trip to Nazareth. They would stay that night in the Sisters of Nazareth Convent, a popular hostel just across from the Basilica of the Annunciation.

Moore had chosen Israel's Galilee region as a focus for the students for several reasons. First, covering all of Israel in a single tour challenged tour parties, not just in the logistics but in the quantity of information the site visits generated.

On a regular adult tour for first-time and likely one-time visitors, Moore generally felt compelled to make the traditional full circuit of Israel, from the southern desert up the Jordan Valley to the Sea of Galilee and northward to Mount Hermon, then around to the Mediterranean Sea coast and back down to Jerusalem. Yet for the youths and young adults, Moore wanted to limit the travel while focusing on the life and ministry of Jesus. Focusing on the Galilee region was a sensible way to do so.

At the time of Christ's earthly ministry, Galilee was the largest of Israel's three regions, the other two regions being Judea and Samaria. Galilee, in Greek and Hebrew variously meaning or referring to a *district, circle,* or *porch*, at first referred to the plain at the northwest end of the region's great inland sea. Israel's king Solomon gave that plain to his Phoenician ally Hiram, king of Tyre along the Mediterranean coastline, for cedar and cypress timber used in the Temple's construction. Hiram despised the gift, calling it the land of Cabul, meaning *good for nothing*.

Galilee did not offer the timber, minerals, waterways, or strategic location that Hiram would have valued as a gift from Solomon. But Galilee did offer a gorgeous inland plain, surrounded by protective mountains and deserts, and watered by sufficiently frequent rains, to make it highly habitable.

In Hiram's time, a thousand years before Christ's advent, non-Jews occupied Galilee. Jews knew Galilee as *the land of the Gentiles*. Hence, the trip of Mary and Joseph to their ancestral Bethlehem at the time of the birth of Jesus. But following the fall of Jerusalem and the Jews' exile to Babylon, returning Jews settled in the relatively peaceful, out-of-the-way region, making Galilee a center of Jewish religious observance, instruction, and life. Young Jewish men could receive high-quality religious training in Galilee, for recruitment into Jerusalem Temple service.

By Christ's advent, the small, inland district of Galilee at the northwest end of the great inland sea had grown in popular reference to include everything from the base of Mount Hermon in the north and the inland sea and its shores, all the way west to the Mediterranean, and south to Samaria. Galilee referred to the whole north of Israel, Samaria to Israel's central region, and Judea to the south beginning at Jerusalem.

Moore's tour still had a lot of ground to cover, to introduce the students to the Galilee region. But it was good ground to cover. Of course, Mary and Joseph raised Jesus in the Galilee region. Yet Jesus also taught most of his parables and performed most of his miracles in Galilee. At about age thirty, he left Galilee only briefly for the Judaean desert south of Galilee, where John baptized the Son of God in the Jordan River.

Christ returned to Galilee under the Spirit of God after his forty days of desert testing. On his return, he traveled throughout Galilee, recruiting and training his disciples, sharing God's word, healing the sick, and doing other miracles, including feeding thousands, walking on water, turning water to wine, and calming the waters.

Moore wanted the students to breathe the atmosphere, feel the soil, hear the sounds, and take in the sights of the Galilee region that Jesus called his home. Moore wanted the students to learn more about Jesus when touring Galilee. But more so, he wanted the students to have a sensory context for what they already knew and later learned of Jesus.

At multiple opportunities throughout the tour, Moore asked the students to consider why God chose Galilee in which to raise his Son. Moore also encouraged the students to consider why Jesus conducted so much of his ministry in the region.

The students discerned that one reason for Christ's Galilee home might have been the region's beauty, welcoming and encouraging so many pilgrims down through the ages. Moore could tell that the most devoted among the students wanted a soft, rich, pastoral home in their heart for the Son of God. At its best, Galilee reflected those home qualities, encouraging the students to dwell in green pastures beside quiet waters.

The students could also see how Galilee's devoted Jewish-returnee community would have been an ideal place to reveal the scriptures' fulfillment in the person of the Son of God. Jews who studied and revered God's word and practiced their faith in heartening and ordering rituals in their relatively isolated communities, might be far more open to Christ's revelation than Jews living, working, and worshiping in more populous and hierarchical, and more strictly governed, regions.

The students also soon appreciated from their study of the region that Galilee's pastoral community of Jewish returnees was a safe distance apart from Jerusalem's concentration of religious, political, and military officials, many of whom were eager to interfere with anyone claiming authority outside of their human institutions, hierarchies, and systems. Early in his ministry, Jesus repeatedly made clear that he preferred that he, his disciples, and those whom he taught and healed should better avoid those authorities, at least until his hour had come.

Through these discussions, Moore also tried to interest the students in what Galilee might mean in its symbolic terms. Galilee was a pastoral district or porch at the foot of the mountains, as God has placed us at the foot of his holy mountain to make sense out of the goodness of his world. Christ's dwelling in that pastoral porch, calming its waters while feeding and healing its people, was God's perfect demonstration of his activity in and desire for the world.

As students continued to gather in the cafeteria, preparing for their first trip north to Galilee, Moore thought again how he wanted the students to leave Galilee and return home seeing their own region and lives in the same symbolism and pattern. Moore wanted the students to carry Galilee in their hearts, receiving Christ's ministrations in their own green pastures, beside their own quiet waters.

Seeing Eva approach stirred Moore from his musing. He rose, smiling, excited, reinvigorated, and looking forward to a kind greeting to kick off the day. Moore scanned the doorway for Helena, expecting her to follow. Eva, though, didn't appear to share Moore's excitement. She instead wore a look of concern.

Skipping a greeting as she reached Moore, Eva asked him, "Can we talk privately before the others arrive?"

"Of course," Moore replied, mimicking Eva's concerned demeanor.

The two moved to a table in the cafeteria's corner, where Eva began speaking in a hushed, urgent tone. She leaned in so that none of the few students spread around the cafeteria would hear them.

"René is in trouble," Eva began. She pursed her lips, struggling with where to begin, while Moore's eyes widened. Moore tipped his head, encouraging Eva to continue.

"He told me some time ago, when we were first getting to know one another, that he'd been part of a unit researching mind control."

Moore raised his eyebrows even further. Moore knew a little about the dark history of U.S. intelligence agency mind-control experiments, coming out of World War II and through the Cold War period. Decades later, a congressional committee had authorized the release of documents of those experiments, some carried out on unwilling and unknowing subjects, to their substantial detriment. Reports further indicated that the methods the agencies learned and deployed had become tools for the trafficking and abuse of many more individuals.

Moore wasn't aware that the experiments were still ongoing. If so, they were likely violating agency assurances to Congress and the public.

"Last night," Eva continued, "He told me he thought he was under some kind of influence or attack, like those he experienced in his former unit when they volunteered as test subjects."

"Was he referring to what happened at the museum?" Moore asked, thinking of the young man's wild look.

"Yes, and two other times so far on the trip," Eva replied.

Moore was about to ask Eva for her thoughts on how to proceed, when he noticed Helena entering the cafeteria.

"Does your mom know?" Moore asked, giving a tip of his head toward the approaching Helena.

Eva shook her head.

"We'll talk," Moore breathed quietly to Eva, as he rose to greet Helena as cheerfully as he could manage in the moment.

Students continued to flood the cafeteria, giving Moore no opportunity to do more than greet them and encourage them to eat so that the group could be on its way to Nazareth. René was among the last to enter the cafeteria, just in time to grab breakfast, while looking more the worse for wear from a night in the dormitory than restored and refreshed.

Moore and Helena soon had the students enter the tour bus in the college parking lot, while the driver stowed their overnight bags. The elderly couple were already aboard the bus and waiting. Eva and René sat together toward the rear, the elderly couple together in the middle, and Moore and Helena on opposite sides of the aisle in the front seats, each joined by an eager student.

As the bus got underway, Moore reminded the students that they would be making a trip quite well known to first-century Galilean Jews, who generally made three annual pilgrimages to Jerusalem, for the Feast of Unleavened Bread (Passover), Feast of Weeks (Shavuot), and Feast of Booths (Sukkot).

Jesus and his disciples, on their several trips from Galilee to Jerusalem and back, would usually have followed the traditional route of devout Jews, up and down the Jordan River valley from the Sea of Galilee in the north to Jericho in the south, just before the Jordan reaches the Dead Sea. That Jordan valley route, taking five to seven days afoot, kept the Jews among their own people, away from the idolatrous stain and greater security risks of traveling through Samaria, lying between Galilee and Judea. Galilean Jews would instead have passed through their own towns of Sepphoris, Nazareth, Tirzah, Shechem, Shiloh, and Bethel.

Yet Moore did not direct the tour bus east out of Jerusalem to Jericho, and north up the Jordan River valley along Israel's modern Route 90. Moore's tour party faced no special corruption or security risks going more or less straight north up Israel's modern Route 60, right through the heart of Samaria. Moore wanted his students to see what Jews know as the *Way of the Patriarchs*, the foothills, watershed, or ridge route that Abraham, Isaac, and Jacob traversed frequently, as the Hebrew Bible records.

Although taking just three days from Galilee to Jerusalem, first-century Jews rarely used the patriarchs' foothills route because of the greater security and corruption risks. Yet Jesus and his disciples did so on a few occasions. Those familiar with the New Testament account of Jesus meeting the Samaritan woman at the well will recall one such occasion. The Samarian route took pilgrims through the towns of Beit She'an, Pella, Sukkoth, and Jericho, and the villages of Bethpage and Bethany.

A third, coastal route also existed, skirting Samaria not to the east but to the west along the Mediterranean coastline. The route, the longest of the three, extended the travel time to a week or more, passing through the towns of Megiddo, Aphek, Lod, and either Emmaus or Beth Horon.

Moore let the students know that on their trips back and forth from Jerusalem to Galilee, they would be taking all three routes. He hoped that in doing so, they would gain a greater sense of the political, religious, military, and security risks ancient Jews faced when traveling within Israel, not to mention the time and effort that traversing the rugged, hilly, dry, and varying lands required.

Moore also wanted the students to see the challenges modern travelers face in traversing Israel. Route 60 straight north from Jerusalem to Nazareth is a nearly three-hour drive, longer than the two hours the eastern and western routes generally require. A part of that longer time is due to the highway's winding route in and out of the hill country it traverses. But a part of that longer time is also due to the four security checkpoints through which the tour bus had to pass to complete the journey.

The checkpoints draw a degree of criticism, especially from those operating vehicles without the appropriate license plate. The checkpoints close sections of the route to Israeli-licensed vehicles, while other sections of the route to Palestinian-licensed vehicles. Vehicles without the required documentation will not pass certain checkpoints. Israel's enforcement of the checkpoints increased after the Second Intifada of the early 2000s, when thousands of shooting attacks on Israeli traffic along the route led to hundreds of civilian casualties.

Although the tour party's students had questions about these modern conflicts, Moore tried to keep their discussions to the ancient scriptural context. At each checkpoint delay, Moore shared with the students more about the differences between first-century Galilee and first-century Jerusalem.

Although Jews resettled Galilee on their return from Babylonian exile, their settlements were within a mixed population. Assyria's eighth century B.C. conquest of Israel's Northern Kingdom had already opened the region to pagan populations, before the exile. The returning Jews formed their conservative Jewish communities, like Nazareth and Capernaum, in and around those pagan populations, including the largely Greek first century B.C. cities of Tiberias and Sepphoris, and the many more Greek towns of the Decapolis south and east of the Sea of Galilee. Jerusalem, by contrast, was largely Jewish, without significant pagan populations.

First-century Galilee also had a purportedly native Herodian prince as its governor, while all of Judea including Jerusalem was under a Roman prefect's rule.

Judeans generally looked down upon Galileans as country bumpkins, influenced too heavily by their Greek neighbors. Judeans, after all, worshiped at Jerusalem's Temple Mount, according to its strict laws, customs, and observances. Galileans, by contrast, worshiped less formally, if they were observant at all. And Galileans spoke an Aramaic dialect that sounded to Judeans like a lazy form of their own vernacular, making Galileans the butt of

Judean jokes. Yet Galileans had rich fishing and farming opportunities that Judeans, living in a dry and mountainous region, lacked, making Galileans generally wealthier than their envious Judean relatives.

Moore encouraged the students to see these ancient differences much as they might experience their own modern differences in regional culture, socioeconomic status, and religious observance. The students found several occasions for laughter over their own perceived differences and those of their neighbors at home.

As entertained as Moore kept the students at the checkpoints, Moore still found time to mull the deep concern Eva had shared with him that morning about René. If, as the young man admitted, he had been the subject of mind-control experiments, then he could have suffered a serious mental trauma leaving long-lasting harm or side effects. Moore felt that the young man needed skilled help discerning what he might have suffered and how it might be affecting him.

But, Moore recalled, Eva hadn't just referred to past experiments. Eva had instead related that René thought that he might be under present attack.

Moore considered the possibility that an agent, foreign or domestic, might indeed be interfering with the young man, by electronic signal, chemical poisoning, or other unknown method or hidden substance or device. Moore had no idea of the sensitivity of the young man's intelligence position, the information he might carry, or the activities in which he might be involved. Moore couldn't rule out the possibility that René had proper concern for an active presence working against him.

Yet Moore had a parallel idea in mind, that René might be under the influence or attack of not just human agents but spiritual entities. Moore held to the scriptural position that the divine realm, or angels and demons for those who prefer, can have both good and bad influence on human thinking and activity. Attacks can be of a spiritual, material, or both spiritual and material nature.

In so thinking, Moore wasn't entering into the realm of little green men or other aliens, trolls or faeries, or other phantasmagoria. He wasn't positing spiritual entities in material terms at all. He was instead simply believing that patterns and principles that clearly influence individuals can have their own emergent agency. Whether you see unbridled passions of the flesh as addictions, psychopathy, or other mental illness, demonic influences, the Greek gods Aphrodite, his sons Eros and Himeros, or Dionysus, or other entities of another realm matters little. Call them gods, demons, angels, or delusions. To Moore it mattered little.

Moore kept an eye on René as much as Moore could during the trip. The young man seemed reasonably attentive when Moore was speaking at the checkpoints but otherwise mostly sleepy, like many of the students. René had given Moore no immediate cause for concern. Perhaps, he thought, the day would pass without another incident. He certainly hoped so.

Yet Moore was unwilling to leave the subject of the young man's mental and spiritual health to its own devices, especially given that René was an agent seeing the possibility that other agents were affecting him, while a part of Moore's tour group.

Moore thus planned to help the young man as much as Moore could with insight into his own spiritual condition and the rescue for it. Moore was, after all, a pastor. He, of all people, should know of such things.

Yet Moore also planned to involve intelligence officials whom he had reason to trust, to protect the young man while ensuring that no foreign agent or intelligence agency harmed René or any other member of Moore's tour party.

At the first opportunity, Moore was going to reach out to his Israeli tour guide friend, to help Moore get in touch with Israel's Institute for Intelligence and Special Operations, commonly known as Mossad. Moore and Eva had already had Mossad's help on their prior Holy Lands trip. Perhaps Mossad would be interested in helping once again.

7

"I need your help," Moore told Helena quietly, as the tour bus neared Nazareth.

At the last checkpoint, Moore had asked the student sitting next to him to switch seats with Helena so that he and Helena could confer.

"René and I need some time to chat," Moore began, leaning in and speaking quietly so that others could not hear.

"Is it serious?" Helena asked, likewise leaning in, concerned.

"Maybe," Moore replied evasively, not wanting to worry Helena or jump to conclusions but also not wanting to leave Helena entirely out of the loop.

Helena looked Moore in the eyes. Putting a hand on his forearm as a signal of both trust and question, she reminded Moore as gently as she could, "You and Eva kept me in the dark last time. Are you sure you want to do so again?"

Moore wasn't sure. In fact, he didn't want to do so. He had doubted last time whether he should have proceeded without letting Helena know his intentions, even though circumstances made it necessary. Moore looked down at Helena's hand on his forearm.

"No," he finally said, "You shouldn't be in the dark. René told Eva that he feels he may be under some kind of mind-control attack. I need to speak with him while you and Eva lead the group at the next site."

Helena nodded. With the same look of concern, she replied, "Is that all you're going to do?"

Moore shook his head, replying, "I'm getting in touch with our old Mossad friends."

After a moment's thought, Helena asked, "Do you think they'll be interested in a single young man's mental state, with everything else they've got going on?"

Moore shrugged, answering, "When they learn he's an intelligence officer, they just might. Especially when they learn that he's connected with our old professor friend."

Helena nodded but replied, "What about Eva? She's an intelligence official connected with the professor, too."

Moore paused. Helena's question had made Moore consider another possibility that he hadn't anticipated. René, Eva, or both of them may already be in touch with Mossad.

When Eva first proposed to Moore that she bring René along, Moore had wondered whether their intelligence agency might be sending René on a mission, perhaps one like the professor's mission following the Russian on Moore's last Holy Lands tour. The agency had used the unwitting Moore once. They might use him again.

Yet that hadn't been the way that Eva had broached the subject with Moore. Eva had said that the two of them wanted to spend time together outside of work. Moore had decided to take Eva at her word. Eva, at least, was innocent of any special operations, even if René might not be.

Moore had also considered alerting his Mossad connection before the trip or on their arrival, explaining that he had two U.S. intelligence officers along. But that disclosure seemed unfair to Eva's innocent intentions and not likely to interest Mossad. So Moore had left the subject alone. Now, though, one of his two young intelligence agents believed himself under attack.

"I need a few minutes with Eva first," Moore finally addressed Helena, explaining, "She needs to know that I'm getting Mossad involved, if they're interested."

Helena nodded. Both Helena and Moore sat back, silently taking deep breaths. Their idyllic Holy Lands tour had just taken an alarming detour. Yet they were just arriving at one of the most idyllic sites of their entire tour. The tour bus pulled into the parking area of the excavated and reconstructed Nazareth Village site, deep in the heart of busy modern Nazareth.

Nazareth is today a bustling city of more than 75,000, with industry, office buildings, residential and shopping districts, fast food, a hospital and healthcare facilities, and most other modern amenities and conveniences. Nazareth is the largest town in Northern Israel. Yet despite its Jewish and Christian history, many regard it today as the country's Arab capital, neither a particularly Jewish nor Christian town.

Nazareth today covers with modern structures and utilities most of the former natural terrain that Jesus would have walked, worked, and enjoyed in ancient times. Nazareth's substantial population today is more than a hundred times what it was when Jesus lived in the village with Mary and Joseph, and his half siblings, among about 500 residents. Nazareth then would have had very few significant structures, likely only a single synagogue and a few residences, none of them especially elaborate. Most of the employment would have been a four-mile walk away in booming Sepphoris.

Surprisingly little excavation occurred in Nazareth until recently. Recent finds, though, have provided clear glimpses into the tiny village Nazareth was in Christ's youth.

Nazareth Village, excavated and reconstructed on one of the few remaining natural sites in the city, attempts quite well to preserve and reproduce the natural character of the village in which the young Jesus grew. Excavations at the Nazareth Village site showed quarrying activity from the Second Century B.C. to the First Century A.D. Quarrying was essential to the so-called carpentry trade of Joseph and the young Jesus, which was more like masonry, given limited wood supplies and abundant available stone. The modern reconstruction shows the quarrying Jesus and Joseph might have done.

Excavations at Nazareth Village also show farming activity from the same period, including farm terraces, spring-fed irrigation, and a wine press. The site's south-facing hillside increased sunlight and provided drainage from the calcium-rich soil, making it a perfect site to grow grapes to supply the on-site press. Wine making was one of Galilee's principal industries. Three watchtowers excavated at the site from the same period emphasize the value of protecting the village's people and products.

The rested students poured excitedly out of the tour bus after their long trip north, stretching arms and legs, and squinting in the bright sunlight of the parking lot. They were eager to explore Nazareth Village's faithful reproductions of first-century residences, synagogue, watchtower, ritual bath, and olive and wine presses, made with original building methods and materials. The students could already see figures dressed in period clothing, moving about the grounds. Before turning them loose on the Village grounds, Moore reminded them of the day's itinerary.

"We'll spend the rest of the morning here, enjoy lunch, and then move on to the nearby St. Joseph's Church, the traditional site of Joseph's carpentry workshop. When enjoying these Village grounds, you may indeed be very near the spot where Jesus learned his father's trade."

Moore gave the students a moment to soak up the impression, before resuming with the rest of the day's itinerary.

"The Synagogue Church is another nearby site we will visit this afternoon, a 12th-century crusader structure that tradition holds was built atop the original Nazareth synagogue in which Jesus worshiped, where the townsfolk at first received but then banished him. That claim may be apocryphal, even though we know that Jesus worshiped in the ancient village synagogue somewhere near the site."

Moore paused again, before concluding.

"We will end the day at the Basilica of the Annunciation, the site where tradition holds that the angel Gabriel told Mary she would bear the Christ child. Our lodgings tonight will be in the nearby Sisters of Nazareth Convent."

Done with the itinerary, Moore encouraged the students to explore Nazareth Village, giving them a few questions to which to try to find answers. Where would they have met the young Jesus if they had just arrived at the village? What would he have been doing, and with whom? The students were soon heading off in twos and threes to explore the grounds.

Helena and Moore remained in the parking lot with René and Eva, speaking of their plans to monitor and engage the students for the rest of the morning, and to gather them for lunch. René soon headed for the restroom. Eva began to follow, but Helena touched Eva's arm lightly to get her attention, indicating that she should remain for a moment to speak with Moore.

"You two go ahead with the students," Moore announced as soon as René was out of earshot. He then turned to Eva, saying, "I'm going to see if René would be willing to have a little chat here at the tour bus before we join you."

Eva nodded, looking to Helena to see if Helena was ready for the morning's supervision of the students. The two had already visited Nazareth Village with Moore and their prior tour party. Both were looking forward to walking the grounds again to imagine themselves living in a town with the young Jesus.

But Moore wasn't done addressing Eva. Taking a quick glance toward the restrooms where René had just disappeared, to be sure that he was still out of earshot, Moore resumed addressing Eva, saying simply, "I'm alerting Mossad of his role and issue."

Eva frowned, promptly replying, "Really? I don't know. That might bring all kinds of trouble. If they think we're up to something, they'll kick us out of the country."

"But you're not up to anything," Moore replied bluntly, with the intention of reading Eva's reaction.

"No, we're not," Eva promptly replied.

Eva's natural response instantly satisfied Moore that Eva was indeed innocent of any intelligence shenanigans. Moore suspected that Eva was a sufficiently skilled actor to convey a natural response when, to the contrary, she had other intentions than those she revealed. But Moore also didn't believe that Eva would deploy those acting skills against Moore, especially not in her own mother's presence.

But Eva wasn't done speaking. Moore's blunt statement triggered Eva's further reflection, just as Moore hoped it would.

"At least," Eva added, "I'm not."

Eva studied Moore's face for reaction, just as Moore had watched Eva respond. Moore looked back, nodding. The two had agreed. René could be on an intelligence mission of which Eva was not a voluntary and knowing part.

"I won't burden René with the knowledge of your Mossad outreach," Eva observed, adding, "He's got enough on his mind."

Moore nodded again. He had gained Eva's assent. If René had a U.S. intelligence operation going, Moore and Eva had just commenced a counter operation involving a foreign agency. Moore hoped that Eva understood the risks and potential complications. Seeing the young man emerge from the restroom area, though, Moore urged Helena and Eva to be off.

"Shall we join them?" René asked Moore cheerily as he joined Moore to watch the two women heading off toward the village entrance.

Moore was glad that the young man looked rested. Moore hoped that the intercession he planned for that morning increased, rather than decreased, the young man's stability and mental and spiritual reserves.

"I thought we might relax and talk for a little bit before we join them," Moore replied in as offhand a manner as he could manage. He added, "It's going to be a long day, and I've had a couple of thoughts I've wanted to share with you since we arrived."

René raised his eyebrows either in interest, mild curiosity, or suspicion, or a mix of all three, Moore couldn't tell. But after a moment's consideration, the young man shrugged, saying only, "Sounds alright."

The two wandered together through the village entrance, where Moore pointed to a bench in the shade of one of the village's reproduction ancient residences. As he and the young man made their way to the bench, Moore had the sense that Joseph might have taken Jesus periodically aside in the same manner Moore was leading René, to share life and learn from one another. The two settled comfortably on the bench, watching the village's period figures walking around the grounds among the visitors.

"You didn't grow up in a religious family, did you?" Moore asked the young man, again off-handedly, while still watching the period figures.

René simultaneously shook his head and shrugged.

"I wanted you to know how much I appreciate that you decided to come along for the trip," Moore continued, adding, "Especially given your unfamiliarity with these things."

When saying *these things*, Moore smiled and made a motion of his hand toward the wandering period figures, dressed in long, heavily worn robes.

Even as he called the young man's attention to the period figures, Moore realized that they made a perfect juxtaposition to how modern minds often regard ancient religious figures. Moderns generally see the ancients as primitive and ancient religious figures as odd or even weird. Yet here these period figures were, moving about like busy ordinary modern citizens, except for their ancient dress. They presented a good lesson, one that Moore was about to draw out for the young man seated next to him.

"We moderns tend to think of religion as an add-on, an overlay to reality," Moore resumed, "Even a set of primitive rituals that we must outgrow and may already have done so fairly long ago."

Moore noticed the young man's wry smile, presumably one of agreement. Moore had set the hook. Time to reel in the fish.

"Yet that's completely the wrong way to think of religion," Moore continued.

The young man's wry smile disappeared.

"Religion is instead a meta language," Moore said, pausing at the phrase before explaining, "Religion frames the cosmos as it is, so that we can think properly about it."

Moore stopped thinking about the young man sitting next to him, who was suddenly listening with greater interest to Moore's psychological and philosophical approach to religion. Moore instead continued on, drawing out his thoughts, trusting that the Spirit was guiding him to speak into the young man's growing soul.

"Religion explains how we explain, how observation, investigation, exploration, science, and consciousness come together in a comprehensible unity, enabling us to live our lives fruitfully, enduringly, to draw out the greatest possible good with the greatest possible purpose and best possible identity."

Moore paused only briefly to let the young man's mind catch up.

"Religious language doesn't describe the world in a modern mind's technical, material sense. Religious language instead describes the process by which we understand the world, in a deep, structural, symbolic sense. Religious symbols reflect the full structure of these relationships, in a language that gives full life to those who understand it and live by it, just as the faith offers and instructs."

Moore paused to look at the young man. René looked briefly back, eyes blank, not thoughtlessly, though, but because the young man was in deep thought. Moore could tell that his words were reaching into the young man's soul.

The young man finally stirred, thankfully with a question, one that Moore welcomed.

"Doesn't science explain away religion?" René asked, his face still blank from deep thought.

Moore smiled, replying in an easy, non-contentious voice, "Religion allows one not only to describe the object, as science might do, but also to recognize how we see the thing as an object, meaning a category or entity with meaningful identity. True science recognizes that it remains embedded within religious forms and understanding, having grown out of the monasteries. The distortion of science, or *scientism*, removes the observer, leaving the observer's consciousness unexplained. Religion restores the observer, thus containing and correcting science, while making science possible."

Moore watched the young man take a deep breath. While René gave no audible response, Moore could tell once again that his words may well have hit their full mark.

Yet it was time to move on to the critical subject. The young man looked as if he might stir and rise, to join the two women in walking the grounds.

René had shared with Eva that he had strangely frightening attacks to somehow face. To help the young man understand and resist those attacks, Moore needed to do more than talk broadly about religion. Moore needed to address the young man's attack. Moore had opened the young man's mind to the true nature of religion. Now he needed to give the young man tools to resist the attacks.

Moore turned to face the young man sitting next to him on the bench. Abandoning his offhand, philosophical manner, Moore addressed René seriously and directly.

"If you don't follow religion's cosmic structure, you have no way of integrating the things that attract and distract you. You also have no way of defending against the things that attack you."

The young man squinted back at Moore. Moore guessed that he might be trying to discern whether Eva had told Moore about the young man's sensation of multiple attacks. Moore knew that he needed to press on quickly to the end, before he lost the young man's attention.

"Allegiance to nothing is allegiance to parasitic processes that divide the soul and bring death. Attach yourself instead to the intersection of heaven and earth, where you'll find a unity of gifts."

"I thought religion was all about moral rules," René replied.

Moore shook his head, answering, "Allegiance and attachment to the highest ideal embodied in the living Christ generates moral action above and beyond moral rules. We receive the gift of life, protection against evil, and meaning, purpose, and identity flowing down from above."

Moore stopped abruptly. Rising, he stretched, smiled at the young man, and asked, "Shall we go find them?"

René nodded. Moore, though, hesitated. Pointing to the two women across the grounds in the distance, while tipping his head toward the restrooms, Moore said, "You go join them. I'll catch up."

As soon as the young man was out of sight, Moore pulled his cell phone from his pocket. Giving it a few swipes, he called his old Israeli tour guide friend, asking for his help renewing their Mossad connection.

8

Most of the students, especially the high schoolers, loved Nazareth Village. The period figures and reproduction buildings, though, put off a few students, as careful and faithful as the curators had been in bringing the ancient village to life. Modern Americans can see many depictions and representations of the life and times of Jesus Christ, in film, television, print, parks, and online. They don't travel all the way to Israel to see more depictions. They go to Israel to see evidence of the real thing.

Moore expected this difficulty. Yet two-thousand years is a very long time. Original sites, especially those in population centers, large or small, ancient or recent, generally lie buried beneath layer after layer of constructions, dirt, and detritus from subsequent generations. For Moore, Nazareth Village, showing a little of the excavated original and a lot more of faithful reproduction, was a good introduction for the students of precisely that difficulty.

Moore chose the next two tour stops, St. Joseph's Church and the Synagogue Church, for their geographic and thematic proximity. Both were but a few blocks away. Each venerated the traditional site of key markers of the youth of Christ and emergence of his public ministry. Unfortunately, neither site had significantly more of the likely original excavations to show the students.

Yet Moore valued the next two sites for a different reason than originality. For two millennia, the faithful have celebrated Christ's advent and ministry through the veneration of the sites, lands, and locations where that advent and ministry took place. The sites may no longer be precisely known or particularly visible. The relics the faithful have claimed to discover, preserve, and display may be authentic or fanciful. But the veneration remains as its own witness to the glory of Christ.

St. Joseph's Church, barely more than a hundred years old, marks a site that since medieval times Christians have treated as the site of Joseph's workshop. It is a small, simple, humble structure, appointed with cut stones like those Joseph might have quarried with the help of the young Jesus. Moore loved it for its humility, dwarfed by the adjacent, extravagantly ornate Basilica of the Annunciation.

The students gathered outside the small church, waiting for Moore's signal to enter. Moore first reminded the students that although their scriptures generally translate the skill and trade of Joseph and Jesus as that of carpenters, the translated Greek and Hebrew word *tekton* applies more generally to a craftsman. Joseph and Jesus more likely worked with stone, like the stones of St. Joseph's Church, as much or more so than wood. Moore then urged the students to enter the church in a silent spirit of worship and reverence, reserving their conversation for when they returned outside.

Helena and Moore stood outside, watching Eva and René enter together, following the students in.

"Eva says it's the first time he's ever set foot in a church," Helena observed to Moore.

"Let's hope that he's carrying the message he received this morning in with him," Moore replied.

Helena nodded, adding, "It's a big moment for Eva, too."

"How so?" Moore replied, already guessing but wanting to hear from Helena.

Helena smiled. Without removing her gaze from the church door into which Eva and René had just disappeared, she reached over, took Moore's hand, and gave it a firm squeeze, communicating far more in that simple action than words could ever have expressed.

The students soon emerged, silently, drifting out, more alone than in the twos and threes in which they had gone in. To Moore and Helena, the Spirit clearly appeared to have reached and moved them. Each seemed to bear the light weight of glory that the Spirit always conveys, even when the Spirit brings a distinct message, attitude, or emotion.

Eva and René were the last to emerge, minutes after the last student. The students waited respectfully in the parking lot, beginning to chat again as the Spirit subsided more deeply in their souls.

Moore stood silent, listening to how the students responded to their encounter with the holy inside the humble little church, bathed in the memory of the honest stone craft of its Author. Some students spoke inanely, unable under the Spirit's continuing influence to fashion clear thoughts. Other students spoke of how the little shelter had moved them. All spoke quietly, reverently, even though they stood in a sunlit parking lot in the middle of a busy weekday. A few students wiped tears.

Eva and René finally emerged. Eva led, with the young man holding her arm. Eva was calm, composed, poised, and serene. The young man was humbled, broken, changed, and relieved, while making no pretense of hiding his tears.

"Everything alright, Honey?" Helena asked gently as the young couple reached them.

Eva nodded. Moore placed a hand on the young man's shoulder, giving it a squeeze of reassurance and respect.

Moore stepped back to announce to the group, "Our next stop, the Synagogue Church, is a short walk away. Let's stroll slowly together, while I share a few things about the site's interesting history."

Moore gave the group a little time to move slowly away from St. Joseph's Church, following Moore in the Synagogue Church's direction. He then began to describe the Synagogue Church's history, typical of similar sites spread throughout Israel.

The Synagogue Church, said to be atop the original synagogue in which Jesus worshiped, is indeed in Nazareth's old market district. Yet the old market district, also known as the district of churches for the Catholic and Orthodox structures that venerate its sacred sites, lies just outside of where excavations have more recently located the tiny ancient village of Nazareth.

The synagogue in which Jesus worshiped, and from which the townsfolk banished him after he announced himself as the Messiah, would almost certainly have been within, not outside of, the tiny village. In other words, the pilgrims who built the Byzantine, medieval, crusader, and later structures venerating the site and other ancient Nazareth sites might have just barely missed their mark.

What archaeologists and scholars can confirm of the Synagogue Church is that crusaders constructed it in the 12th Century, about the same time that they constructed a nearby Church of the Annunciation. Their intent was to commemorate and protect the two holy sites, the former where Jesus worshiped and taught, and the latter where the virgin Mary learned that she would bear Jesus.

The crusaders had some basis for believing that they had sited the two churches accurately. In the case of the Church of the Annunciation, crusaders built it atop an earlier Byzantine church said to mark the annunciation site. Catholics recently replaced the crusader Church of the Annunciation structure, Pope Paul VI having dedicated the new Church of the Annunciation in 1969. The process of tracing structures back is how archaeology generally proceeds when attempting to locate original sites.

The claim to originality of the Synagogue Church differs, though. It relies, wholly or in large part, on the testimony of the interesting sixth-century Christian figure the Pilgrim of Piacenza. The famous pilgrim from Northern Italy claimed, in one of the last writings before the region's Muslim conquest, to have seen at the site not only the Roman-era synagogue in which Jesus worshiped but also the Hebrew Bible from which he read and the bench on which he sat.

Unfortunately, the Pilgrim of Piacenza has a reputation among scholars as a notorious embellisher. That reputation doesn't make him unusual for early pilgrims and later crusaders who, after all, traveled long distances at great effort, expense, and peril, in hopes of discovering and preserving sacred Christian sites, and in some cases retrieving sacred Christian relics. One finds those claimed relics spread throughout Italy and in other European locations.

Romans vanquished the Jews in Jerusalem, throughout Judea, and in the Galilee region, in the Jewish War and rebellion beginning in 66 A.D. and culminating in the Temple's 70 A.D. destruction. Conquering Roman forces would very likely have destroyed Nazareth's tiny synagogue, just as they destroyed the Temple and countless other Jewish sites. Later generations could have rebuilt the small Nazareth synagogue for the Pilgrim of Piacenza to discover, leaving some possibility that the Pilgrim had found the correct spot. But in this case, excavations haven't confirmed that supposition, leaving the site's originality in question.

Moore stressed to the students that those issues should not substantially detract from their appreciation for the Synagogue Church. The Synagogue Church is its own testament to remarkable pilgrim devotion.

The students soon reached the site, gathering inside a small courtyard with entrances to not one but two churches. Ahead, a small door led down seven steps to the underground Synagogue Church, its depth helping to mark it as an early, 12th-century construction. At the courtyard level to the right was a larger door to the Greek Catholic Church of the Annunciation, a humbler version of the nearby, significantly larger and more-ornate Basilica of the Annunciation, making the greater claim to be the annunciation's location.

Moore encouraged the students to descend into the Synagogue Church, having very much the simple stone character and feel of St. Joseph's Church, which the students had just visited. The Synagogue Church, though, being a crusader rather than modern construction, is many hundreds of years older than St. Joseph's Church. Its ancient humility thus naturally appears more authentic than designed and contrived.

Students entered a few at a time, staying only a few minutes before emerging to let others enter. Moore peered through the Synagogue Church's small door and down the steps, to watch the students running their hands lightly along the cut stones, neatly arranged to provide for an altar, small, raised platform for the bishop to address the assembled worshipers, two arched niches, and other spare adornment. A tiny window high inside an arched stone alcove, but from the outside right down at street level, let a slit of natural light into the womb-like sanctuary.

Eva and René were the last to enter, staying only briefly minutes while the waiting students chatted in the courtyard. Moore could see that their brief descent into the underground church didn't have the same impact of their St. Joseph Church visit, even though the students were appropriately reverential, inspired, and moved.

Moore had expected that difference. Each successive church they visited that day, and the several other successive sites they visited that week, would likewise have different and often lesser impacts. The students had filled their spiritual tanks quickly. Each successive tour stop would simply be topping those tanks off, as the impact of each visit drained slowly into the students' souls.

The waiting students peeked into the street-level Greek Catholic Church of the Annunciation. As they did so, Moore explained to the waiting students that Nazareth today holds as many as eighteen churches of the annunciation. Several claim to venerate distinct annunciation-related sites. One claims to be over the cave that was Mary's Nazareth residence. Another claims to be the site of the spring where Mary first heard the angel Gabriel's voice. Another claims to be the site of the residence where the Spirit overcame Mary.

While the students would visit only two annunciation churches, those two churches inspired the students to remember, reflect upon, and deeply appreciate Mary's extraordinary role in bringing the Son of God into the world.

With the long day wearing on, Moore gathered the tour party for their last destination before retiring for the night to the Sisters of Nazareth Convent. They would visit the most prominent annunciation church, the Basilica of the Annunciation, right across the street from the Convent.

As the students approached the Basilica on foot, led by the animated Moore, its mammoth size and elaborate contemporary design stunned them, surely the effect its noted modern Italian architect and Catholic Church funders intended. It was the largest Christian church in the Middle East when completed in 1969.

The Basilica's soaring dome appears like an inverted lily flower, especially looking up from the huge sanctuary inside. The lily, a symbol of Mary's purity and Christ's innocence, opens down over the traditional site of the angel Gabriel's announcement to Mary and Mary's simple but glorious acceptance, marked deep below the huge, modern sanctuary. A great lamp stands atop the dome's pinnacle, marking the Light that came into the world. Scripture inscriptions, huge mosaics, colorful painted panels, carved reliefs, and statutes adorn the inside and outside of the modern structure.

The extravagance with which the Basilica of the Annunciation marks and celebrates the traditional site contrasts sharply with the humility of the claimed original site far beneath. Standing in the courtyard outside the impressive structure, Moore helped the students trace back its connection to the original site.

The Catholic Church built the modern Basilica of the Annunciation after demolishing a church that Franciscans built on the site in the mid-1700s. The Franciscans had purchased the site in 1620 from its Muslim Arab owner, taking a century plus to acquire permission to build a church. The Franciscan purchased the site because of its ruins of a crusader church, destroyed with the fall of the crusader kingdom in 1187, claimed to have been built over the annunciation site. The crusaders had, in turn, built their church atop the ruins of a first church on the site, traced to around the year 427.

That was as much as the site's Catholic owners knew of the site's provenance, until excavations for the modern Basilica of the Annunciation. Those excavations revealed ancient silos, cisterns, and cave dwellings below the earliest church. They also revealed a synagogue church, earlier than the church constructed in 427, with a pillar bearing, in Greek, the inscription *Hail Mary*, the archangel's very annunciation to Mary. Little wonder that the site makes the most prominent claim to originality.

Moore let the students explore the Basilica's vast upper sanctuary, examining the ornamentation along its walls, while peering up at the enormous inverted-lily dome. He then led the group down a staircase to the Basilica's lower level, where the Basilica's builders carefully preserved the remains of the earlier churches on the site.

One end of the lower room, far smaller than the grand church above, opened to a sunken grotto marking Mary's traditional cave home. Stones, pillars, and other remnants of the earlier churches flanked the grotto's opening.

An altar stands deep inside the grotto, its Latin inscription reading *Here the Word was made flesh*. An ancient mosaic floor just aside from the grotto's entrance identified the deacon of Jerusalem whose gift paid for the site's preservation, perhaps by converting Mary's cave home into the site's first church. Moore once again let the students explore the lower room, including its treasured grotto.

As extraordinary as the site was, the students didn't linger. It had already been a long day, filled with emotion. Moore soon gathered the students for their retreat.

Outside again in the Basilica's courtyard, Moore directed the students to one last site, adjacent to the grand Basilica of the Annunciation and adding further credence to its originality claims.

As they moved to the neighboring site, Moore explained that in 2009, excavations for a new Mary of Nazareth International Center uncovered what the Israel Antiquities Authority described as the first confirmed residential building from the ancient Nazareth village existing at the time of Christ. The new Center preserves and displays that residence.

The students were able to view the plain dirt floors of two small rooms, surrounded by the spare ruins of stacked stone walls. The preserved site had a tiny courtyard with a cistern to collect rainwater. Whether Mary ever dwelled in that specific residence or not seemed at the moment to make little difference to the students. The ruins clearly depicted the humility with which Mary, Joseph, and Mary's child Jesus must have lived.

Moore took the moment to remind the students that while Jesus came as the world's King of kings, he came as an entirely different kind of King.

The last thing that Moore and Helena had to accomplish in their long but full day was to help the students retire to the neighboring Sisters of Nazareth

Convent. That time elicited more favorite moments of the day.

A few of the students had expressed quiet concern whether the Sisters of Nazareth Convent would provide the amenities they needed to rest and recover from the long day. Those students had an image of a convent as a place deprived of comfort, perhaps even of sustenance. Yet Moore had chosen the Convent for its clean and comfortable, if simple, sleeping quarters and its sustaining dining-room fare. Its appearance immediately relieved the students of any concern upon their arrival.

Moore had also chosen the Convent for its traditional Nazarene building design and materials, and the views it afforded of the old Nazareth structures packed tightly around it. Moore wanted the students to rest, even to sleep, in the humility and richness of the moment, conveyed so perfectly by the grounds and churches they had visited throughout the day. Moore wanted the students to soak in the memories and emotions of their day.

With the help of Eva and René, Moore and Helena ensured that every student received their room assignment and key, located their room, left their night bag, and returned to the dining area for a late meal.

Helena could see that the students had developed a rhythm and the relationships to support it. The students were satisfying Helena's maternal instincts, for which Moore was especially appreciative. Moore always felt comfortable helping youth and young adults explore the Holy Lands sites. He was far less in his element when helping youths and young adults meet their needs for sustaining society and conveniences.

The exhausted students retired after the evening meal, without lingering. Eva and René joined them. Helena and

Moore looked at one another with exhausted smiles, after the last of the others had left.

"Are we making a good team?" Helena asked.

Moore nodded, with a deepening smile.

The next day would test their teamwork.

9

Moore and Helena met early in the Convent's dining room the next morning, enjoying quiet cups of coffee together. Moore explained that he planned to let the students gather their wits a bit before heading out on the tour bus for the day's next exciting stops. Helena was all for it. The day before had brought a sea of sensations, rush of emotions, and flood of information.

Once the students had joined them and begun their breakfasts, Moore rose to address them, first asking how well they had rested and how they were feeling. Looking around the dining area, Moore saw nods and smiles, and heard a few pleasant affirmations.

Yet Moore instead caught a look of concern from Eva. René sat next to her, looking blank, exhausted, and distressed. Moore raised his eyebrows in question at Eva, who shrugged. Moore signaled discretely that they'd talk. Eva nodded. Moore's quick glance at Helena confirmed that she, too, had gotten the picture and subject of shared concern.

"Then let's have some observations and questions from yesterday before we turn our attention to today's exciting tour," Moore again addressed the students, ignoring for the moment the young man's distraught condition. Perhaps, Moore briefly thought, René just needed to let a good breakfast settle.

The first few students to raise hands and speak shared favorite spots and moments. Other students chimed in, agreeing and amplifying the comments.

Moore was not surprised that Nazareth Village and St. Joseph's Church seemed to draw the strongest reactions. He was also not surprised that the mammoth, modern Basilica of the Annunciation drew no comments, even though it had clearly impressed the students when they were at its site late the prior afternoon. Moore had long observed that the humblest, most original-seeming sites tended to draw the deepest, most emotional, most positive reactions.

Soon, though, a student raised a hand with a question about the Crusades, saying, "We kept hearing yesterday about crusader churches. Back home, everyone seems to mock the Crusades. What really were the Crusades?"

The question, like the students' other observations, did not surprise Moore. His tour party members, young and old, often had such questions.

Moore began by suggesting that the Crusades involved highly complex social, religious, and political motives and movements. That complexity, Moore suggested, is why modern Americans either have no clear view of the Crusades or may have strongly negative views. Moore suggested that one's view of the Crusades, like one's view of other historical developments and events, especially those involving religion, may depend more on one's own perspective than on objective assessments.

Moore asked the students what positives and negatives they drew from the bits and pieces of archaeology and information they saw and heard the day before, involving crusaders. Predictably, the students gave a wide range of positive and negative views, the positives having mostly to do with preserving and venerating Christian sites, while the negatives having mostly to do with the impact of those efforts on local populations.

Moore made sure that students understood some of the social issues and political interests lurking behind the Crusades, even while highlighting the religious motives on which they drew and the religious conflicts they reflected and fueled. His goal was simply that the students appreciate the movement's complex mix of good and bad motives, good and bad results, so like most human endeavors.

Moore also encouraged the students to suspend judgments on the Crusades while in Israel, so that they could better absorb their first-hand observations. The students would have a lifetime to process, research, and analyze those observations, to form whatever conclusion they felt most appropriate. Moore wanted the students to adopt a reflective stance, not a judgmental one, at least while on the ground in the Holy Lands.

Their discussion had done the trick. Moore could see that the students were awake, refreshed, and eager to head out for their next explorations. It was time to move forward.

"Today's itinerary will challenge us in a different way," Moore resumed addressing the students. He explained, "Yesterday, you saw settings for Christ's holy conception, how in his youth he would have learned his Joseph's carpentry trade, and where his first preaching occurred. Today, you'll see where he may have worked with Joseph on Herodian structures, from which he may have drawn context for his teaching. We'll then make our first visit to the shores of the Sea of Galilee, where we will stay in a hostel for the night."

The tour bus was soon on its way, the students eager for the day. Eva, Helena, and Moore had no chance to confer regarding the distressed appearance of René, although Moore looked for the opportunity. The short ride to Sepphoris, a little north and west of Nazareth, was quickly over.

Jesus did not mention Sepphoris in the teaching and preaching the New Testament records. He did, however, frequently refer to *hypocrites* in his parables and lessons. In its day, the term Jesus used came from the masks that theater performers used. Those performers in effect wore two faces, the one they presented to their audience and their own quite-different face hidden behind the mask.

Nazareth, Capernaum, and the other Jewish towns and villages in which Jesus grew up, resided, and taught did not have grand theaters where skilled performers wore masks. Observant Jews would generally have avoided Greek and Roman theaters.

Sepphoris, though, as the seat of Galilee's ruler Herod Antipas, held a grand theater seating about 3,000 spectators. Antipas, Herod the Great's son, constructed the theater and many other grand edifices in the years Joseph was teaching Jesus construction and craftsman trades in tiny Nazareth, an hour's walk from Sepphoris. Scholars put Christ's frequent use of the *hypocrite* illustration together with Joseph's trade, need for employment, and proximity to the only significant construction projects in the area, to speculate that Jesus helped his father work in Sepphoris, perhaps even building its grand theater.

The tour bus made its first stop for the day at Sepphoris' excavated and partially reconstructed theater. Moore explained these suppositions to the students as they sat on the theater's stone seats, possibly wrought by the strong bare hands of their Savior.

Moore soon shared other significant Sepphoris sites with the eager students. Backed by Herod Antipas' riches, Sepphoris was an arts and artisan community. Excavations have uncovered examples of the beautiful, carved-stone pillars that lined its streets and supported its structures, and the elaborate mosaic floors.

Romans and other gentiles were not the only beneficiaries of these ancient structures. After Rome destroyed the Temple in 70 A.D. and vanquished the Jews' religious leaders, Sepphoris in western Galilee became the Second and Third Century seat of rabbinical Judaism. The Romans spared the Jews in Sepphoris in recognition of their refusal to join the Jerusalem revolt. The Jews moved the Sanhedrin to Sepphoris after the Temple's destruction.

To illustrate the rich Jewish life of Sepphoris, Moore took the students to a site of an excavated and well-preserved Sepphoris synagogue, sporting an elaborate and beautiful mosaic floor. Moore made sure to point out to the students that the mosaic included detailed images illustrating the astrological zodiac, including images of Helios, the Greek god of the sun.

The students rightly questioned whether the Hebrew scriptures would sanction zodiac references. Depending on its interpretation, the Torah may instead condemn astrological practice. Moore suggested only that the rabbinic Jews' late incorporation of astrological images into Jewish religious depictions showed how effectively the Jews could preserve their core beliefs while navigating foreign culture and customs.

To illustrate Sepphoris' cosmopolitan nature, Moore took the students to another major excavated Sepphoris site, possibly of its long-ago city hall. The site sports a mosaic floor of Egypt's Nile River emerging from the mouth of a woman, Alexandria's city gate and lighthouse, one of the famous seven wonders of the ancient world, and female Amazon warriors. If Jesus visited and worked in Sepphoris with Joseph, he would have encountered a worldly culture. Even if he didn't visit Sepphoris, Jesus would have known of its influence across Galilee, on Jews and Gentiles alike.

Helena pulled Moore aside at their last Sepphoris site, while the students explored the excavated ruins. She motioned for Eva and René to join them.

"What's up?" Moore asked once the four of them were together. He glanced cautiously at René to assess his condition. The young man looked slightly confused, if no longer distressed.

"We're not sure it's anything," Eva replied with a concerned look. She turned to René, waiting for the young man to speak.

René shrugged, saying, "I had a dream last night, more like a nightmare. I've had them before, as we all probably have. But this one seemed different, more of a foreboding."

The young man shrugged again, as if in apology for even raising the subject.

"Anything specific?" Moore asked.

René shot a glance at Eva, still apparently unsure of whether to elaborate. Eva gave him a quick nod.

"Well," the young man reluctantly resumed, "It involved the abduction of young Jewish children from some sort of a seaside commune."

René shook his head, as if to dismiss the thought as senseless. Moore, though, raised his eyebrows in concern. Moore hadn't mentioned to anyone yet, not even Helena, that their next stop was to be at a kibbutz along the Galilee shore.

"Anything else?" Moore inquired of the young man, who shook his head firmly in a similarly apologetic manner.

"Hey, thanks for sharing," Moore said, putting an encouraging hand on the young man's shoulder. He added, "Stretch your legs and clear your head for a few more minutes before we reboard the bus for our next stop."

Eva shot a glance at Moore, who nodded slightly, signaling Eva to draw the young man away while Moore and Helena conferred. As soon as Eva and René were out of earshot, Moore turned to Helena.

"I've got a call to make," he said, pulling his cell phone from his pocket.

"What's up?" Helena asked, concerned at Moore's urgent tone.

"Our next stop is Kibbutz Degania at the south end of the Sea of Galilee," Moore replied, watching to see if Helena understood the concern. Her widening eyes showed Moore that she did indeed.

Moore swiped at the cell phone before lifting it to his head. Within a couple of quick minutes, he had related the young man's dream and the tour group's itinerary to the person on the other end of the line. Moore stood holding the phone to his ear, listening for another minute before briefly acknowledging whatever the speaker had said. He let the phone down, tapping its screen to end the call.

"Let's get the students on the bus," Moore said, turning toward the direction of the ruins the students were still exploring.

"Any change in plans?" Helena asked, following Moore's steps.

Without pausing, Moore shook his head, saying, "No, we're to proceed as planned."

"That doesn't feel right," Helena replied, placing a hand on Moore's arm to pull him to a stop.

Helena looked at Moore, waiting for his reply. Moore, though, couldn't form a reply. He had his instructions. Finally, the words came to mind.

"He said they can't be chasing after dreams," Moore told Helena with a shrug.

"So they're doing nothing?" Helena asked with a hint of frustration leaning toward anger.

Moore shook his head, replying, "I didn't say that. I'm hoping that my call instead puts them on high alert. I don't think he would have said so, though, either way."

Helena nodded, releasing Moore's arm. But she pursed her lips in dissatisfaction.

"We don't have to go to the kibbutz, do we?" she asked.

"I don't know," Moore replied, adding with another shrug, "His instructions were to proceed, though. It may be important to the children's protection that we go."

Helena took a deep breath. Moore knew why. She was thinking of the safety of her child Eva and her many adopted children, the youth and young adults of their tour party group.

"Come on," Moore said, taking Helena's hand, "We're a good team, remember?"

Helena gave Moore's hand a squeeze before they headed off to round up the students.

The drive from Sepphoris due east to Kibbutz Degania at the Sea of Galilee's south end took under an hour. The tour bus reached the sea at Kinneret and headed south the last couple of miles along the seacoast to the kibbutz, where the sea empties into the southward-headed Jordan River. They were at the very south end of the Sea of Galilee, directly across from the sea's north end where Jesus moved to reside and teach after leaving Nazareth. Moore's plan over the next couple of days was to work north along the seacoast.

First, though, Moore wanted to introduce the students further to Jewish life and culture along the great inland sea. Kibbutz Degania seemed to Moore like the perfect place to do so.

Moore had found over his years of leading Holy Lands tours that his American guests knew little if anything about Israel's kibbutz movement. Kibbutzim are unique to Israel. Traditionally, they are a collective community based on arduous land recovery and agrarian development, carving fertile land out of Israel's dry and rocky wildernesses.

Kibbutz Degania, the site of the mid-day visit of Moore's Holy Lands tour party, was the historic first kibbutz, founded in 1910. *Kibbutz* means *gathering.* Young Jews had gathered at the relatively desolate location to drain the area's swamps for homes and farming. Their hard labors and shared devotion to one another worked brilliantly. Kibbutz Degania and other kibbutzim have been economic engines for their regions and significant innovators within their farming sectors and industries.

More recently, kibbutzim have indeed diversified into manufacturing and other fields and industries. Kibbutz today even support tourism, by establishing and operating popular kibbutz hotels and offering museums. Moore's students were soon exploring Kibbutz Degania's Gordon House, with exhibits on the area's natural history, earliest human settlement, and kibbutz founding and development.

While kibbutzim began with a primary focus on wilderness or other unused land recovery, kibbutzim now also work on urban and suburban redevelopment. Some kibbutzim have also strayed from their socialist roots to support private ownership.

With more than 270 kibbutzim in Israel, supporting nearly five percent of Israel's population and up to ten percent of its economy in the farming sector, kibbutzim remain a significant social, cultural, and economic influence within Israel.

Kibbutzim have also long had an outsized political and military influence. Kibbutzniks comprise about fifteen percent of the members of Israel's Knesset, its parliament. Israeli war hero Joseph Trumpeldor, founder David Ben-Gurion, and military legend Moshe Dayan were all kibbutzniks, indeed all participating in Kibbutz Degania. Moshe Dayan was the second child born there. And when Ben-Gurion retired as Israel's prime minister, he took up residence at a Negev Desert kibbutz Sde Boker, both for its solitude and to retain the kibbutz movement's influence.

Moore made no effort to hurry the students through Kibbutz Degania's Gordon House exhibits. Moore himself found the natural history museum's exhibits of the flora and fauna of the Jordan River valley to be fascinating. Moore found equally fascinating the exhibits on the Galilee region's earliest settlements and their methods of fishing the sea out of which Christ called his catches, and farming the hillsides and plains on which Christ taught. The students shared Moore's enthusiasm, lingering over the exhibits.

Moore, Helena, and the students also found enchanting the kibbutz grounds, on the gorgeous inland sea, hard along the equally beautiful Jordan River. Helena, especially, encouraged the students to wander around the grounds, sit by the sea and river, and breathe the sweet air, carrying the fragrance of both dry desert and sunlit waters.

All the time, though, Moore was keeping an eye and ear open for signs of trouble. Moore soon realized that he had no way of detecting any such sign. He didn't know how anyone might abduct children from kibbutz grounds. Moore wasn't naive. He was aware that kibbutz abductions are an unfortunate possibility in Israel, both surrounded and populated by neighbors hostile to Israel or its Jews.

Moore also kept an eye and ear open for signs of Israel National Police or Mossad special protection, and for kibbutz security personnel. But again, Moore wouldn't have known where or for what to look. Nor did he want to concern René or the students, or tip René off to the fact of Moore's secret Mossad contact.

In midafternoon, after the students had time for a refreshing and relaxing seaside lunch on the kibbutz grounds, Moore discerned that it was time for the group to reboard the tour bus for their next destination. It was only then that he learned of a successful security operation.

"Heard the news?" the tour bus driver asked Moore, as Moore stopped by the tour bus to check to see if the driver was ready for the students to gather and board. The driver had the bus door open, while he sat relaxing in the first seats behind the driver's seat.

Moore, standing halfway up the bus steps to peer at the lounging driver, shook his head, asking, "What news?"

"The INP foiled an attack late this morning," the driver replied.

"Where?" Moore asked, blankly, without revealing his concern.

The driver gave Moore an irritated look, replying, "Here. Right outside the gates. Didn't you hear the sirens?"

Moore shook his head. He hadn't heard a thing. Nor had any of the students mentioned anything. They must have been in the museum, engrossed in the exhibits.

"The INP must have had a tip off," the driver continued, adding, "Otherwise, they would have been nowhere near here. We might have seen dozens of abductions or murders. They might have even murdered me and commandeered our bus."

The driver shook his head, muttering what Moore assumed was a Hebrew epithet Moore did not recognize.

Moore took a deep breath, asking the driver, "You good to go?"

The driver nodded, rising slowly from the seat and stretching.

"Better watch out for your students," the driver muttered, adding, "I'm hoping your group wasn't a target of the foiled attack."

10

As soon as the students boarded the tour bus at Kibbutz Degania, word spread among them of the foiled kibbutz attack. The news frightened the students, who to that point had kept Israel's ever-present security concerns at arm's length.

Moore might have preferred to address the issue once they reached the relative security of the nearby hostel where they would spend the night. But the students' nervous chatter called upon him to make some statement.

"We should be very thankful for Israel's security forces," Moore began, saying the only thing he could think at the time. To ensure that the students had more context, he explained, "The Israel Defense Forces work closely with the Israel Police and Israel's national intelligence agency to keep its citizens and visitors secure. Crime statistics suggest that we are generally far safer here than we might be in most major American cities."

Students had a few questions, most of which Moore was unable to answer. He did, however, reassure the students that they would be staying the night in a city the Jewish population of which made it as secure as virtually any place in Israel. Moore also indicated that while the foiled attack was certainly alarming, the Galilee region had not been facing any recent unusual conflicts that might be likely to generate further attacks. If the contrary had been the case, Moore assured the students that he would never have brought the students to the region.

The news of the foiled attack rattled Helena, Eva, and René even more than it did the students. The students had no premonition of the attack. They thus regarded their proximity to it to be a complete fortuity, pure chance rather than nefarious design. Moore, Helena, Eva, and René, though, had to consider the extraordinary circumstance of the young man's prophetic dream. Moore, Helena, and Eva further had to consider how the secret communication of that dream must have contributed to the foiling of the attack.

Sitting next to Helena on the tour bus, Moore could tell how unsettled, alarmed, and confused the prophecy and event had made her. The foiled attack had given Helena a much greater concern over proceeding with the trip than Helena had expressed to Moore that morning. Yet Moore felt helpless in trying to comfort, console, or otherwise aid her, even by making a clear decision. Moore felt that he needed first to speak with his Mossad contact before taking any alternative action. Moore just hadn't had a chance yet to do so. All he knew he should do was to get the students safely away from the kibbutz.

That Helena knew that Moore was at a loss in the moment to help her simply compounded Moore's own frustration. Moore and Helena had, in other words, reached the first point in their relationship where each felt unable to help the other nor to help themselves. Their leaning on one another, encouraging one another, or advising and guiding one another simply wasn't possible under the circumstances. They had instead to let the Spirit work within their silence and trust.

Moore took a deep breath before saying to Helena in the seat beside him, "We'll be at the hostel in a few minutes. I'll consult my contact then, from which we can consider options."

Helena winced slightly, giving no other reaction.

Moore correctly read Helena's non-response as further frustration that Moore did not just turn the tour bus toward the Tel Aviv airport to get them all out of there. For a moment, Moore considered telling Helena why he thought they needed to reach and retire at the hostel, to give Moore time to consult and plan. But seeing the stress on Helena's face convinced Moore that if he did so, they might find themselves in their first good argument.

Within about twenty minutes, the tour bus had pulled up at the David Hostel in the seaside town of Tiberias, seven miles northwest around the southwest shore of the Sea of Galilee. Tiberias lies about halfway up the sea's western shore, at the base of rising mounts sheltering the seacoast along that stretch.

Moore had chosen the modest David Hostel, across from a supermarket in a residential district high on the hillside town, for its home-like setting. Its mix of small rooms, dormitories, and indoor and outdoor living spaces seemed to Moore perfect for making the students feel at home in a Jewish city.

For the moment, the modest, home-like hostel deep inside a large Jewish city, also seemed to Moore like a secure setting. He noticed Helena's apparent relief, once the students had piled from the tour bus and tumbled into the hostel to choose and settle in their rooms.

Tiberias held quite a bit of significant history, if fewer specific scriptural sites. Moore thus didn't plan extensive tours for the students within the city. The hostel would, though, serve well as their Galilee home away from home, assuming that Moore and Helena determined to continue with the trip.

Moore indicated to Helena that he was going to disappear for a little bit to make his security contacts. Helena agreed to take any students who were interested across the street to the supermarket where, with the help of the hostel's generous hosts, she and the students would acquire dinner fixings to prepare back at the hostel. Nearly all the students soon headed out with Helena and Eva, happy at the chance to engage in a simple domestic chore in one of Israel's key Jewish communities. The few students who remained crashed in their rooms or lounged in the living areas.

René, too, stayed behind. Moore let the young man know that he would soon join him on the hostel's rooftop patio. Moore then retired to his private room to make his security call.

"No phone communication. Meet me outside now," Moore's contact answered abruptly, as soon as Moore's phone made the connection. The call ended before Moore could reply.

Rising from the bed on which he had perched to make the call, Moore took a deep breath, shook his head in the mysterious way that intelligence agents operated, and headed for the hostel door.

Stepping out into the small parking area behind the hostel, Moore instantly saw the familiar, unmarked, dark sedan with heavily tinted windows. The sedan's passenger-side door swung open, inviting Moore to enter. Moore strolled quickly over, hopped in, and shut the door. The Mossad agent with whom Moore had worked on his prior Holy Lands trip sat behind the sedan's wheel.

"Glad to see you so near," Moore said with a smile of greeting.

"You got our attention with your prophetic call," the agent replied.

"Well," Moore deferred, "The dream wasn't mine, but I'm very glad you took the call."

"Indeed," the agent replied, "It would have been a massacre or mass abduction without the notice."

The agent, though, wasn't interested in small talk. He simply continued, saying, "Where's the young man?"

"Inside," Moore replied, adopting the agent's stern, matter-of-fact tone, while adding, "He and I are meeting privately as soon as I'm done here."

The agent paused to consider, before asking, "How's he doing?"

"I don't know," Moore answered frankly, playing the agent's own hide-and-seek game, "Not until I speak with him."

The agent ignored Moore's sleight. Moore continued with his question, asking, "What do you recommend we do?"

"Proceed as you planned," the agent said bluntly, adding, "Don't tell anyone of our contact."

"The young woman and her mother already know," Moore replied.

Again, the agent ignored Moore's disclosure. He simply added, "And let me know the instant the young man shares anything at all out of the ordinary."

"What are your plans?" Moore asked, knowing his question wouldn't elicit a straight answer.

The agent looked across at Moore. Moore detected the slightest smile, which Moore correctly construed as the agent's appreciation for Moore playing along with agency games.

"Call me," the agent repeated, indicating with a subtle tip of his head that Moore was to exit the vehicle.

Moore opened the door, turned, and began to climb out. As he did so, he heard the agent's voice behind him say, "We won't be far."

Moore smiled to himself as he shoved the sedan's door closed behind him. Every profession has its culture, language, professional demeanor, and norms. He understood intelligence agents, even if they were a breed apart.

René was waiting for Moore on the rooftop patio when Moore mounted the stairs a minute later.

The young man was in a different mood and predicament than Helena, one that Moore felt like he might be able to help the young man address. Unlike the (Moore hoped) momentary strain in his relationship with Helena, Moore felt strangely equipped to counsel the young man.

"Strange day, huh?" Moore greeted René, who looked up at Moore with a wan smile.

Moore took a seat alongside him. The two looked out over the dense tangle of residence rooftops toward the sunlit sea, a glimpse of which they could just make out. Tiberias lies on a hillside above the seacoast plain, giving much of its residents a view or at least glimpses of the historic, beautiful, and at times intensely serene body of water.

"Am I losing my mind?" the young man asked, looking down again at his hands, which he rubbed and clenched in anxiety.

"Maybe," Moore replied, waiting for the young man to look up at Moore's teasing smile. Satisfied from the young man's wry half-smile that the young man understood that Moore was jesting, Moore began, speaking in a reflective, almost pensive manner.

"We lose our minds when our categories shift from the fitting juncture of the somatic and spiritual, the intersection between the transcendent and the material."

Moore waited to see if the young man was in a mood to pursue his meaning.

René looked up again from his hands, saying only, "Explain."

"Oh, our sanity always hangs in that delicate balance between our humanity and divinity," Moore repeated, continuing, "Push too far either way, toward human material alone or toward the metaphysical alone, and you'll find trouble."

"What sort of trouble?" the young man asked, still looking down at his hands.

"The horror of nihilism the material world alone offers," Moore replied, "Or the horror of sorcery, magic, and the underworld the transcendent alone conjures."

The young man looked up at Moore again, grasping the pastor's meaning but more scared than comforted by the proposition. The young man shuddered, saying, "Like walking a highwire, always ready to fall."

Moore shook his head, replying, "You can look at it like that if you wish the anxiety and confusion that come with it. Or you may choose instead to see it as it is, gladly falling from secularism's highwire act into the wide-open arms of the Son of God."

The young man looked up, raising his eyebrows, having made another connection he hadn't considered before.

Seeing so, Moore added, "His perfect humanity and divinity, we naturally and supernaturally pursue. He has already made the perfect balance. We need only accept it."

René tipped his head, asking with another soft chuckle, "So that's the Savior's role?"

"One way of seeing him," Moore replied, adding, "He reminds us how we bring meaning and material, the spirit and the body, together. Without each in the right balance, we suffer. Christ reunites in us the human and divine, so that we see and understand again, rather than losing our souls or minds."

The young man gave Moore a puzzled look, asking, "But how does he do so? Even if he was God in person, he was still just one being, among millions or billions of beings."

Moore smiled. Nodding, he said, "Yes, that's the mistake lots of us make. But Christ wasn't just one person, one being. He was being itself."

Moore watched with satisfaction the young man's stunned look, nearly like someone had punched him in the gut. Moore had hoped that the young man would understand and appreciate what Moore had just said.

After a moment's pause, Moore resumed, saying in a sympathetic tone, "You're likely feeling the sort of horror any sane person in your situation would feel, after a nightmare nearly came true. Horror comes not from fear but from looking into the aperture of non-meaning, when the bottom falls out of the tenuous foundation on which the psyche attempts to stand alone, unbalanced, without a fruitful accord between the spiritual and somatic."

René huffed in wry appreciation for Moore's assertion, saying only, "Tell me so. Until today, I've never had a nightmare that nearly became real."

"I wouldn't worry about anticipating rare events, even frightening ones," Moore observed, adding, "Warning was the role of the prophets of old, those who dreamed dreams and saw visions."

"But what if another one comes true?" the troubled young man pressed Moore.

Moore paused for a moment. He then rose and, with a small smile of consolation, said, "Tell you what. How about if you just tell me the instant you have another dream or vision. Your last one worked out alright."

The young man looked up at Moore, asking, "You mean my dream was part of the solution rather than the problem?"

"Seems so to me," Moore answered with a reassuring smile, adding, "Better that the prophet stands on the wall giving his warning. Others may then figure out what to do."

René shrugged, nodding.

"Come on," Moore said, encouraging the young man to rise, "Dinner's cooking."

Helena and the students had indeed returned from the supermarket. René and Moore found them in the hostel's kitchen happily chatting, chopping, stirring, and going about other dinner preparations, while other students talked and played games in the living areas nearby. A home-cooked dinner was soon served to the enjoyment of all.

As students finished their dinners, Moore began sharing with them the rich history and spiritual significance of Tiberias.

Tiberias was barely more than an empty seaside plain and hillside at the time of Christ's advent. The Hebrew Bible's book of Joshua mentions the ancient small village of Rakkath at the site. The site had several mineral hot springs that from earliest times attracted human use for healing baths.

In 20 A.D., before Christ began his public ministry, Galilee's local ruler Herod Antipas, son of Herod the Great, determined to settle the site as his region's capital, resettling thousands of Jews among the extravagant palace and other public structures he built. Recent excavations uncovered a 7,000-seat theater on the site. Herod wisely named the city after the reigning Roman emperor Tiberius under whose rule Herod held sway. Tiberias was thus a prominent new regional capital by the time Christ began his public ministry in around 30 A.D.

Yet given Herod's Roman devotion, Tiberias was a pagan rather than religiously Jewish city throughout Christ's earthly ministry. Leading Jews even refused Herod's orders to resettle there, claiming that a cemetery in the city made the city unclean for Jews.

Moore pointed out to the students that Christ, too, avoided the city, whether for that reason, to delay conflict with Roman authorities until his proper time had come, or for other reasons. Worldly rule wasn't the Savior's immediate mission. The New Testament mentions Tiberias only once, as the place from which boats had sailed across the Sea of Galilee to its where Jesus fed the five thousand.

The crowd used the boats to return not to Tiberias but to Capernaum along the sea's northwest coast.

Curious about their capacity for symbolic reasoning, Moore asked the students what they thought was the meaning of the boats. His question drew mostly blank stares, confirming Moore's suspicion that the students were still developing their capacity for such insights. But one student soon answered that the crowd's encounter with Jesus had turned the course of the boats from a pagan city to Christ's adopted Galilee home. Moore smiled, agreeing.

Moore resumed, explaining that Tiberias became much more important to Jewish leaders after the Jewish Wars of Roman rebellion led to the Temple's 70 A.D. destruction and Judea's desolation. Galilee became the center of Jewish life, and Tiberias a seat of significant influence. For hundreds of years, Tiberias was Galilee's largest Jewish city, where rabbis compiled parts of the Mishnah, or Oral Torah. Jews came to regard Tiberias as one among four Jewish holy cities, the others including Jerusalem, Hebron, and Safed

Tiberias remained populous and influential as a caliphate capital during early Muslim rule. Earthquakes and Egyptian Mamluk conquering and rule gradually reduced the population and influence of Tiberias. But in 1880, Jews began returning to the city, so that by the 20th century, the city had once again grown. Today, it is again a significant commercial, residential, and tourist center for the Galilee region.

The students' meal ended with Moore's suggestion that they take the evening relaxing at the hostel. They'd had two long, eventful days. Moore wanted to add that they would explore Tiberias in the morning. But he first needed to speak with Helena, updating her on his contact with Mossad.

Moore joined Helena and several students in the kitchen, helping to clean up from dinner. Soon, the students drifted off, leaving Moore alone to speak with Helena. Helena continued cleaning the kitchen, ignoring Moore, as Moore watched.

"I met with Mossad," he finally said.

Helena stopped, turning to Moore to ask, rather more coolly than Moore had hoped, "What did you learn?"

"They're staying near," Moore replied, hoping Helena would appear reassured.

She didn't. Instead, she asked, "What does that mean?"

Moore shrugged, shaking his head and replying, "They never say. But they want us to immediately report anything he dreams or foresees. And they want us to proceed as usual."

"Are you satisfied with that?" Helena asked, her tone indicating that she might not be.

Moore shrugged again. To match Helena's mood more than indicating his own feelings, he replied, "Not entirely."

"Me, either," Helena agreed. She laid a hand on Moore's hand, atop the counter.

"So, how shall we proceed?" Moore asked.

"A morning exploring the city, and then onward, I suppose," Helena replied, adding with a roll of her eyes, "Unless René has another dream tonight."

The two shared a brief laugh, a team once again.

11

"Very little is true," Moore found himself replying to a question that René had asked him as the two strolled the Sea of Galilee waterfront.

The night had passed peacefully for all, including the young man. Helena had taken the female students out to explore Tiberias, with the help of Eva and the hostel's female proprietor. Moore had taken the male students out with the same intent, with the help of René and the hostel's male co-proprietor.

For a number of reasons, Tiberias lacks substantial excavated ancient sites. Earthquakes devastated the city several times, leaving little of ancient structures to discover and preserve. What ruins remained might be fifty feet below the material that earthquakes and later construction deposited atop them. Conquerors did their own part in the city's further devastation. Moore could have led the tour party to various sites of interest around the city, such as the preserved foundation of a crusader church, two Ottoman-era mosques, and several old synagogues from the 18th and 19th Centuries. But those sites would have contributed little to the overall tour.

Instead, within a few minutes, both groups, one led by Helena and the other led by Moore, had ridden a city bus to the bustling restaurant and tourist district along the Galilee shore. Tiberias is easy to explore on foot, aided by a city bus service. The city's small harbor and restored waterfront is a popular tourist site. Urban development after 1967's Six-Day War between Israel and a coalition of Arab states opened up a waterfront promenade, lined with shopping, eateries, and other tourist attractions.

Moore usually avoided consumer attractions on his Holy Lands trips. But he felt that the youth and young adults might appreciate a breather from the at-times intense emotions, explorations, and studies of the ancient sites. As he and René watched their young charges poke through the shops and study the attractions of the eateries, Moore felt that his judgment had been right.

The ease and enjoyment of walking along the Tiberias waterfront and modest harbor seemed to relax René, too. That was when the young man asked Moore a question about what was true or not about the world, about life, about faith.

As Moore and René walked on, watching the students explore the eateries and shops, Moore explained to the young man his response that little is true.

"We tend to think of truth in material terms," Moore shared, "As in whether our beliefs align with so-called facts. We regard facts as accurate surmises, assertions, inferences, or descriptions that we make about what exists in the material realm, often supported by our examining technological instruments, whether microscopes, telescopes, or laboratory tests. Truth, we tend to think, grounds itself in these accurate descriptions of the material realm."

"Sounds about right," René replied as they walked on along the waterfront.

"But that approach is an extraordinarily limited, historically naive, and largely unhelpful view when making necessary sense of life," Moore replied. He added, "Indeed, it really doesn't address truth at all. It disguises and confuses truth through a distorting and disarming lens."

The young man raised his eyebrows and tipped his head in surprise, waiting for Moore to explain. He didn't have to wait long.

"Descriptions of material conditions that fail to take the observer into account cannot be true in any meaningful sense," Moore resumed, adding, "They purport to explain what's out there without accounting for the observer's existence, perspective, and influence on those conditions."

René shook his head, saying, "I'm not getting it. I need an illustration."

"Well," Moore replied, with a gesture toward the bright sky, "Consider the sun. Our technology tells us that it is a mammoth gas fusion factory that will one day consume the earth before collapsing in on itself to a smothering death."

The young man smiled, saying, "Sounds about right."

"Sure," Moore agreed, "But it says nothing meaningful whatsoever to the ordinary observer who asked the question. That answer ignores the obvious and enormously important phenomenon of the sun to the ordinary observer, in favor of a meaningless distortion. While the description might well be accurate if one were to travel to the sun or far into the future, neither of which is at all possible, the description is instead pointless or, worse, misleading for the one who asked the question."

René smiled, saying, "I see the point."

Moore resumed, "Don't see truth as out there somewhere in these constantly changing and largely unpredictable material conditions, only for others with peculiar instruments to define. Truth must instead account for the observer. Truth must answer the observer's question as to the subject's meaning."

The young man thought for a minute as they paused outside one of the shops the students had entered. He finally asked, "What does Christian faith say about truth?"

"Hah!" Moore replied, making sure René understood his appreciation for the question and its astounding answer, "Christ himself says that he is the truth."

"Yes," the young man replied, with a tinge of disappointment, explaining, "I've heard that, but it never made sense to me."

"But you've just seen how truth must account for the observer," Moore answered, adding, "Christ's statement that he is the truth does precisely that."

"How so?" René asked.

"We account for both material reality and its observer only at the intersection of material and meaning," Moore replied. Eager to explain, he continued, "Christ is both the Word or thought, that rationality that you experience when trying to discern truth, and the Word's materiality, the flesh-and-blood body for which truth must answer to adequately represent reality. When Christ said that he is the truth, he also said that he is the word and the life."

The young man smiled, shaking his head and saying only, "Pretty intense."

"Oh, it's the passion of Christ, alright," Moore seconded the young man's instinct, adding, "He is the author and force of life itself."

René chuckled. Holding up a hand, he joked, "Enough! Enough!" giving the two of them a good laugh together.

Moore's group of male students soon rejoined Helena's group of female students along the waterfront.

"So, what's next, Chief?" Helena greeted Moore brightly, buoyed by her waterfront walk with the young women.

Gathering the full group around him, Moore pointed to a beautiful wooden boat moored in the harbor and replied, "We have a sea excursion planned. We've only got to decide whether to head back to the hostel for lunch to be on the water this afternoon, with swimsuits if it warms up enough, or instead to grab snacks here and head out this morning while it's still cool."

A brief debate settled the question. The students would repair to the hostel for another home-made meal and then return to the waterfront suitably attired for an afternoon boating excursion with a potential swim.

A city bus had the tour party back at the hostel in no time. Helena and several students dove into the supermarket for simple lunch fare, while Moore, René, and the rest of the students prepared for the afternoon. In little more than an hour, the students had eaten, rested, refreshed, and changed for afternoon outing.

A city bus had them back at the waterfront a few minutes later. Moore led the tour party back to the point where they'd meet the boat captain for the excursion. The students stood on the wharf, pointing at the boats and chatting, while Moore used his cell phone to call for the captain, whom he'd expected to meet at the wharf.

"Hey, pastor?" René called quietly to Moore who, having finished his call to the captain, was watching the students point and chat eagerly about the boats moving in and out of the small harbor.

Moore looked at the young man with a smile, hoping he had a question or comment about their morning discussion. But Moore's smile quickly faded, seeing the strange look on the young man's face. Moore turned in the young man's direction to walk to his side and put a kind hand on his shoulder.

"You alright?" Moore asked.

"I think so," René replied, "But could you do something when the captain arrives?"

"Hang on a second," Moore replied, seeing the captain walking crisply toward him wearing a big smile.

Moore turned to greet the boat's proprietor with a manly hug. The two slapped one another on the shoulder, joking and laughing with one another about their changing appearance, each seeming to the other to have aged slightly since their last boating excursion together.

Sea of Galilee religious tour boating is a considerable small industry for the region. Israel draws well over four million international tourists each year. That number is only a tiny fraction of the tourists visiting the top three worldwide tourism destinations beginning with France and including Spain and the U.S. But Israel's tourism concentrates in Jerusalem and Galilee. And Galilee visitors are often not satisfied staring at the gorgeous sea. They want to go out on the waters as the disciples did, thinking of the miracles their Lord did on the sea.

Moore had used several boat excursion operators over the years. Some companies had several boats of varying sizes and reproduction originality to New Testament times. Other individual proprietors had only one boat. Moore had found nearly all of the operators helpful and all of their excursions worthwhile. But the excursions also differed significantly.

Moore's favorite captain was among those with but a single vessel. In fact, the captain had built his own vessel, attempting a relatively faithful reproduction to the times. The vessel was neither large nor small. It perfectly fit Moore's typical tour parties of around twenty guests.

Moore's favorite feature of the vessel was that the captain had fitted it with an electrical engine that made the trips surprisingly quiet, even serene, where the guests heard little more than the peaceful lapping of the water against the hull.

The quiet of the captain's electrically powered vessel had another advantage that Moore expected the students to especially enjoy. Back at the hostel over lunch, Moore had let the students know that the captain would invite them to play their favorite music, or most-fitting music for the excursion, over a bluetooth speaker system he had installed. Moore's disclosure had sent the students into a frenzy choosing and sharing worship and popular songs, and vocal and instrumental arrangements.

Another reason Moore liked his captain friend's excursions over the outings other proprietors offered was that his captain friend had no canned spiel. Because the captain was the only one who operated his vessel, he had no need for a script to share with other employees. Each time that Moore had been on the waters with his captain friend, his friend had shared his unprecedented knowledge of the sea in a different arrangement, including different information.

Indeed, as the students soon discovered, the captain tended to wait for questions and then answer the questions more in a discussion format than lecture format. He was also warm, kind, and funny. That the captain was also a Christian gave Moore an additional level of comfort in hiring him for sea excursions.

Israel identifies itself as a *Jewish democratic state*. In so doing, Israel at once marks its majority Jewish population and Judaism faith, while simultaneously suggesting a guarded commitment to ethnic and religious diversity. Despite that Judaism is the nation's declared faith, Israel is a relatively diverse society, from the standpoint of both ethnicity and religion. Jews comprise around 74% of Israel's population, while Muslims comprise around 18%. Christians and Druze each comprise less than 2%. Israel's parliament, the Knesset, typically has a dozen or more Muslim members.

Moore didn't mind at all that the tour bus drivers and various other guides and connections on whom he relied for his Holy Lands tours were often Jews and sometimes Muslims. He'd even had a couple of Buddhist and several atheist or agnostic service providers. Moore felt that his Christian tour party members could gain useful insight into the region's history, conflicts, cultures, and faiths, through interaction with non-Christian service providers, some of whom were Moore's good friends.

Yet the Sea of Galilee excursions that Moore led were so emotional, inspiring, powerful, and sentimental, for so many of his tour party members, that having a Christian captain conduct the tours seemed, in Moore's experience, to make them all the more reliable and special.

With Moore's blessing, the captain began organizing the students to board and settle into his boat. He was already making small talk and joking with the students, putting them at ease about the excursion, while raising their anticipation for a moving afternoon, one that might further involve a little fun.

Moore, though, turned his attention to René. Moore hadn't forgotten the young man's request that Moore do something when the captain arrived.

"How can I help you?" Moore asked René, thinking for a moment that the young man might have some concern with boating safety or otherwise going out on the water. Moore even wondered if it was possible that René might not be able to swim. Moore had other tour party members make confidential disclosures of the sort to him in the past.

"Could you check to see that the captain has a working fire extinguisher aboard, and adequate life preservers, too?" René asked.

Moore's eyes widened. Trying to discern the young man's cause for concern, and thinking that perhaps René himself was a boater who routinely took such precautions, Moore stammered, "Well, of course. Care to explain?"

The young man shrugged, shaking his head while looking down to kick absentmindedly at the boards covering the wharf. But at that moment, Moore realized what he'd been trying to avoid. The young man had some premonition of impending disaster.

"Did you dream of something?" Moore leaned in close to René to ask.

The young man wagged his head back and forth with a frown across his face, indicating that he had not dreamed but that something had nonetheless alerted him to a concern.

"René, tell me," Moore insisted quietly but firmly.

"I'm not sure I can," the young man replied, still shaking his head and kicking at the wharf boards. Taking a deep breath, René looked up into Moore's face, struggling to articulate what he was experiencing.

"A fire on the water," the young man said in halting words, almost unintelligibly, with a bit of the wild look Moore had seen René exhibit only once before.

René looked away, shaking his head, saying, "I know it makes no sense." He looked back at Moore again, adding in a pleading tone, "Just check for a fire extinguisher, please?"

With that, the young man turned sharply away to join the students boarding the ancient-looking boat.

Moore pulled his cell phone from his pocket, giving it a swipe or two before lifting it to his head to say a few spare words into it. Listening for a moment to the reply, Moore slid the phone quickly back into his pocket to head for his captain friend, who had just helped the last person, Helena, aboard.

"Can you do me a favor?" Moore asked, drawing the captain aside out of earshot of the students chatting excitedly aboard the boat.

Helena watched Moore and the captain converse, quickly, quietly, and earnestly. Moore looked to be trying to convince the captain of something to which the captain was reluctant to agree.

When they were done, the captain climbed smartly aboard. Moore followed. Without a word to anyone, the captain headed straight for the pilot's station, where he opened a cabinet below the wheel, withdrawing a fire extinguisher that he held up for Moore to examine.

When Moore nodded, the captain stowed the fire extinguisher back in the cabinet. The captain then picked up a microphone, flipped a switch on the wheel's console, and handed the microphone to Moore. Helena could just barely hear the captain saying to Moore with an annoyed look on his face, *You tell them.*

Moore took the microphone, explaining to everyone aboard that they had life vests stowed under their seats and to please don them for the excursion's duration. Moans went up from a few of the students, to laughter from others. Everyone respectfully complied, as the captain prepared to push off the wharf. Moore helped untie and throw aboard the craft's lines before jumping back aboard himself.

As the board drifted silently back under its electric motor, the captain asked with a big smile, "Who's got the music?"

Students' hands shot up, sparking a gay debate over the first choice of music. Soon, though, the students had music wafting happily across the sea's still waters.

Moore settled into a seat in the stern alongside Helena. From the moment that the two had agreed on the trip, each had looked forward to the moment when they would be back out on the Sea of Galilee again together. But neither had the sense that they had anticipated with such relish.

Moore was alert, thinking of the actions to take if he saw any sign of smoke or fire. Helena was waiting for Moore's explanation of the fire extinguisher inspection and the life vests announcement. And Moore was not looking forward to sharing that explanation.

Once they were underway across the water, Moore took a deep breath and turned to Helena, prepared to explain. But to his surprise, Helena shook her head, even giving Moore a small smile.

"It's alright," she breathed, adding, "I understand. And we're in good hands. Let's enjoy every moment."

Looking deep in Helena's eyes, Moore nodded slowly. As he did so, he found his eyes beginning to water in appreciation for the profound trust Helena was showing, not only in Moore but in her maker.

Back on the wharf, a slender, austere, female figure, one whom Eva and René would both have recognized if she had wanted to show herself, watched the craft pull away across the waters. And back among the shops and eateries lining the wharf, Moore's Mossad agent contact watched the slender female figure.

12

"What do you call this body of water?" one of the students asked the captain. The student had seen roadside markers and onshore signs give the Sea of Galilee different names. The student also knew her Bible.

"You are now out on the Jordan River," the captain said with a big smile, teasing the students.

The captain stood at the wheel toward the rear half of the boat, using the microphone to save his voice, even though the boat was small enough for a raised voice to be heard over the water lapping its hull. Most of the time, the students simply enjoyed the excursion, listening to their chosen music over the boat's bluetooth speakers. Whenever the captain spoke, usually in answer to a student's question, the captain would expertly turn the music down, leaving its quiet rhythm as a backdrop to his chatter with the students.

When Moore had first pointed out the boat the students would board for their afternoon excursion, Moore's choice of craft had pleased the students. The students had seen several tour boats, none as original looking as the captain's own. That original look meant the boat's hull was fashioned of long wood planks, with elegant curves gently rising to a finely pointed bow.

The boat didn't have the ancient, soiled sails some students might have envisioned. The disciples would have sailed the lake, not piloted their craft with a modern electric motor, like the captain did, standing at his wheel. And the captain had equipped his boat with a pleasant little canopy covering most of his guests, all but Moore and Helena sitting under the sun in the open rear of the craft. But the graceful curves of the boat's hand-crafted hull, slicing easily through the water, made it a beauty to behold and pleasure to ride.

The captain had designed and built his boat based on a highly reliable pattern of the fishing boats in use in the 1st Century A.D., when Jesus walked on these waters and his disciples fished them. In 1986, drought exposed more of the lake's northwest shore, allowing locals to discover remarkably well-preserved remains of the wooden hull of a first-century fishing boat. Many call it the *Jesus boat*, although only its time and location give any indication of its potential connection with the Lord and his fishermen disciples. The captain built his boat, as far as he was able, to that boat's specifications.

The captain gave the students a moment to see if any understood his quip, when he gave his jesting answer to the student's question about the lake's name.

Seeing nothing but looks of puzzlement, the captain explained, "The Jordan River begins well to the north of this body of water, spills into it, traverses it, and spills out at the southern end, to make its way to the Dead Sea. In that sense, you are in the Jordan River. Anyone for a baptism?"

A few students laughed at the captain's joke, while others, still adjusting to the captain's jovial manner, wondered whether his offer was serious.

"We'll pause for a swim later," the captain answered his own humorous offer. He then answered the student's question about the lake's name.

The disciples and other ancient Jews and Gentiles of their day knew the northern region of Israel to the west and north of the great lake as *Galilee*. They thus would also have known the body of water as the *Sea of Galilee*. But astute readers of the Hebrew Bible and Christian New Testament know that the lake has borne other names, particularly Lake Kinneret or the Sea of Kinneret. Hebrew-speaking Jews in Israel today, and Muslims and others with roots in the region, are likely to call the lake by that name.

The *Kinneret* name itself has a confused origin. The Torah and Book of Joshua name a town Kinneret near the lake's northwest shore, between latter-day Capernaum and Magdala. No town of that name exists at that site today. A modern village by the same name Kinneret instead lies along the lake's southwest shore, between the kibbutz the students visited at the lake's south end and Tiberias, halfway up the lake's western shore. But that modern village is not the ancient Kinneret, which instead lay all the way up the lake and to the northwest. The modern village did not lend its name to the lake.

The ancient Kinneret was at a strategic location, between the productive inland sea and its fertile plain, emerging between hilly terrain to the northwest. Excavations of the ancient Kinneret site have confirmed a significant Bronze Age settlement, predating the Israelite settlement of the site, one that Joshua granted to the Naphtali tribe. Indeed, an ancient Ugaritic text, older than the Hebrew Bible, mentions the city Kinneret at the site.

The students nodded in appreciation of the captain's encyclopedic knowledge of the lake. The captain developed and shared that knowledge carefully, fruitfully, knowing that he plied the lake for a living in a sort of fishing like that Christ had long ago offered the disciples. But the captain wasn't quite done answering the question about the lake's name. After teasing and joking with the students, the captain resumed his answer, as the craft slid silently out toward the lake's middle.

By New Testament times, the ancient Kinneret had become *Gennesaret*, another name the gospel accounts give to the lake and to the ancient city near its northwest shore. Jesus and the disciples may have used that name, although they would also have referred to the region and perhaps at times to the lake itself as *Galilee*.

Scholars today disagree about the ancient origin and meaning of *Kinneret* and the associated *Gennesaret*. Some say that the lake's harp-like shape, wider at the top than the bottom and leaning to the west, traces the name's origin to an Ugaritic word for a harp or similarly shaped musical instrument. Others say that the *Gennesaret* name comes from Hebrew words for a guarded or watched valley. Interestingly, the Jerusalem Talmud, written well after Christ's earthly ministry, traces *kinneret* to the ancient name for the fruit-bearing thorn trees of the region, later known as Christ's thorn jujube, or to the lake's cane reeds.

When the captain concluded, the student who had asked the question piped up, saying, "But the lake also goes by *Tiberias.*"

The captain smiled and nodded in appreciation for the student's reminder. When the captain asked the student where the lake got its *Tiberias* name, the student promptly answered that the name must have arisen when Herod Antipas named and resettled his capital Tiberias along the lake's shore during Christ's young adulthood. Moore and the students had, after all, already discussed the origins of the city Tiberias.

As the boat motored silently well out onto the lake, with only the sound of music and lapping water filling the air, the students began to marvel at the lake's great size. Picking up on the students' interest, the captain explained that the lake is just over eight miles across at its widest point and fully thirteen miles long, quite a sizable freshwater body. The disciples would have traversed about thirty-three miles if they had walked all the way around it. Their fishing boats would have had about sixty-four square miles of lake surface to ply.

Looking over the craft's side, one of the students asked how deep the lake was. The captain answered that the lake's depth is about 141 feet at its deepest point, although the lake's level has varied both historically and recently. The lake's level depends in part on rainfall and snowmelt from the mountains to the north, feeding that part of the Jordan River that empties into the lake's north end.

Precipitation is not the lake's only source. Underground springs also feed the lake. But those springs are not as pure as the rainwater feeding the lake from the north. The springs feed some saltwater into the lake. The lake retains its fresh waters by the weight and pressure of the rain-fed lake limiting the flow of the salt springs underneath. A low lake level and less weight and pressure from above means the springs feed the lake with more salty water. Tiberias city officials, drawing the city's freshwater from the lake, recently demanded a desalination plant when low lake levels elevated salt content.

More recently, the lake's level has also depended on the extent of farmland irrigation the national managers of the lake permit, using the lake's waters as a source. Irrigation at one point drew the lake's level significantly down. Israel, though, has been a world leader in desalination efforts, turning salty seawater into fresh water for farming and other human use. Those efforts, and a huge desalinated Mediterranean tunnel project, may soon produce enough fresh water for the lake's managers to maintain normal levels.

The lake's managers continue to monitor lake levels daily, careful to preserve the lake's extraordinary freshwater qualities for use and enjoyment by many. Competition among Syria, Jordan, and Israel for the lake's freshwater, and freshwaters drawn from the lake's northern sources, complicate that management. Israel provides nearly two billion cubic feet of the lake's waters to Jordan annually under a treaty between the two nations.

The captain ended the discussion of the lake's natural features by indicating that lake levels have variously exposed or covered significant historical sites along the shore. He assured the students that their tour guide Moore would doubtless show the students some of those sites and mention their discovery when lake levels receded. The captain also mentioned that the lake had once been part of a much larger inland sea and that it is the lowest

The students saw no evidence of fish or other marine life in the lake, although they had seen fishing boats in Tiberias' harbor. One of the students asked the captain the kind of fish the lake offered and how much fish the boats caught.

To remind the students of the fishing on the lake that several of the disciples once did and that has spanned more than two millennia, the captain began his answer with the so-called *St. Peter's fish*, as the locals know it. St. Peter's fish is a Galilean species of tilapia that often leads the annual commercial fishing catch. That annual catch, though, has varied greatly from year to year, between as much as 300 tons to as little as under 10 tons, due to overfishing and other natural and unnatural cycles involving water level, salinity, and the condition of shoreline plant life for fish breeding grounds.

Local fishing boats also seek commercial catches of other types of tilapia, both natural and introduced, as well as species of sardines, catfish, and ray-finned fish, with varying success depending on the stresses affecting those fish populations. Overfishing, destruction of natural habitat along the shoreline, and other stresses have led to the fear that some species, no longer seen at all, are extinct.

Sad note, but the captain reassured the students that the lake's managers have continued to address the several issues impacting fish and other lake life.

At one point, one of the students pointed out a great bird making its way slowly across the lake's expanse. The captain identified the bird as a gray heron. He then used the opportunity to briefly describe the lake's significance for local and migrating bird life. The Sea of Galilee supports year-round populations of francolins and griffon vultures. Waterbirds wintering on the lake include teals, grebes, herons, egrets, cormorants, and gulls.

The captain had soon tired both himself and the students of their discussions. The captain noticed the students' restlessness. They had sat patiently while the boat made its way well out onto the lake and toward its north end. The captain flipped the boat's electric motor off, letting the boat drift.

The captain looked back at Moore and Helena in the boat's stern, asking, "Time for a swim?"

Moore looked at Helena, shrugging. Helena nodded.

"Let's see if we have any takers," Moore replied to the captain, having gained Helena's assent.

Within minutes, several students had taken the plunge. A ladder the captain hung over one side of the boat's stern, and many helping hands, aided the students' entry into and exit from the cool lake waters. The swimming students splashed the students aboard the boat, taunting them gaily, but without much success, to join them.

The swimmers were soon back in the boat, towels wrapped around them. The captain let the boat continue to drift. Captain, students, Helena, Eva, and René all looked to Moore, expectantly.

Moore knew that these Sea of Galilee excursions were a natural high point for Holy Lands tours. He knew to plan something worshipful to mark the event, although he also took care not to force the moment. Just being out on the lake, thinking of the extraordinary events that occurred there, might feel sufficient. Yet soon, well aware of the moment, Moore rose to speak. The captain offered Moore the microphone, which Moore declined, instead standing beside the wheel's console to address the students.

"I hope you'll remember this moment for a lifetime," Moore began, adding, "Indeed, eternally."

Moore took a deep breath, holding a serene smile, nearly closing his eyes. Shaking his head softly with the glorious weight of the moment, he swept an arm across the lake vista.

"Take a look around you," Moore urged the students. He continued, saying, "See this exquisite creation for what it is, whom it hosted, what happened on its waters, and what those events mean to us, indeed what they communicated to the world."

Moore took another deep breath. He thought less now of the students listening to his words, as they looked across the lake's serene expanse, and thought more of his incomparable Lord. Letting the students see how his inward eye had turned from them to their maker, Moore no longer addressed the students but instead spoke in prayer.

"Father, you invited your Son to walk across these waters, proving him to be above your creation, as your creation's eternal master. Your Son stilled the storm on these waters, showing him to be the master not just of space but also of time and circumstance. Your Son drew sustenance for his friends from these empty waters, showing him to be our nourishment and our provider. Your Son walked up the mountain alongside these waters to dwell in prayer with you in your unfathomable and unknowable darkness. And your Son walked down the mountain alongside these waters to rescue his friends from their drowning death, as he rescues us and all those who wish to know and honor him."

Moore knew that he could have continued to speak to his Lord and preach to his Holy Lands guests for the rest of the afternoon, into the evening. He wanted his conversation with Christ to go on forever. Where better to begin and commemorate that conversation than on Christ's own waters? Yet Moore felt in the moment that he needed to stop, to let the students in on his conversation.

Thus, with tears in his eyes, and overcome with the emotion of the moment, Moore invited, "Whoever wishes to continue in prayer, please do so."

Moore eased himself back to his seat in the boat's stern, alongside Helena. Helena put a gentle hand on Moore's arm, as Moore settled into the seat beside her. Silence hung in the boat's air, no student wanting to be the first to break the rich spell of the moment. But soon, students began to pray aloud, one by one.

Some of the students' prayers were short, others longer. Some spoke timidly and quietly, others boldly and confidently. Some prayed for families and friends, others for communities or causes, and others for themselves and their own relationship with the Lord. In time, the prayers slowed and then stopped. Moore prepared to rise again to close the prayers, expecting that the captain would then pilot the boat to shore in good spirits for the evening.

Yet then, just before Moore closed the prayers, a young man's voice arose. René, the ostensible agnostic, began to pray.

"Father, I am learning about you, learning that you are not who I thought you were but are instead far greater. I feel that I am just meeting you, while also beginning to see that I need you and that I owe you. I also hear and believe that your Son, on whom I now newly rely, has already addressed what I owe you. Please accept me now, and please continue to open my spiritual eye to you."

Eva, eyes shut, listened intently, as did Helena and Moore. The students may not to that point have been aware of the young man's faith exploration. But the young man's prayer opened his exploration to them. Eva, Helena, and Moore each silently prayed that God would indeed do as René had asked, while they also prayed that the students would come around the young man gently and sensitively.

Moore rose, thanking the Father for hearing their prayers. Some students stood to stretch. Others turned to their seatmates to share friendly chatter. The captain moved to the wheel, preparing to start the engine for shore.

René rose, too. He moved to Moore who still stood in the boat's stern to whisper a request. Moore looked at the young man, stunned but with a growing smile. He clapped the young man on his shoulder and then gave him a hearty side hug.

"Hold on a minute," Moore said with a huge smile to the captain at the wheel, "We've got one more baptism to complete in the sea's Jordan River."

Students clapped and cheered, while René stood blushing but smiling. Eva rose, moved quickly to the young man's side, and joined Moore in hugging him. Helena, too, rose to join in their embrace.

"Wait, wait," one of the students shouted, "We've got music for the baptism!"

The student held her cell phone aloft as the boat's bluetooth speaker began picking up its signal to blare the popular rock baptism anthem *Holy Water*. Students stood, singing, cheering, and dancing to the music that shot across the waters in grand celebration.

To the students' delight, Moore was the first over the stern and into the water in a great splash, out of which he rose to beckon René to join him. The young man leapt over the stern in another great splash. The two tread water while Moore gave the baptism creed. And then Moore supported René as the young man let his head sink slowly under the water.

An instant later, the young man's head popped back up, his face wearing a huge smile, as the music and students' song rang across the water and up into heaven.

13

"Do you smell that?" Helena asked Moore with a look of concern.

The two were seated in the stern of the boat again. The captain stood at the boat's wheel, wearing a serene smile as he piloted the boat back toward shore. The students, seated forward in the boat, were quiet in their reverie and afternoon stupor, listening to instrumental music from the boat's speakers caressing the waters.

The impromptu baptism of René in the Jordan River hidden in the sea's expanse had enchanted the party. The students were now intoxicated with the quiet joy of the

Holy Spirit who had descended when the baptism opened heaven, briefly uniting earth and heaven.

This God whose Spirit brings serene comfort and deep joy was a new phenomenon for René, who had until then only heard of a false god who brings nothing but rules with their violation's inevitable condemnation. Moore's gentle correction, the elderly couple's less-gentle prodding, and the vitality of Christian youth and young adults surrounding him had softened the young man's heart and opened his blind eyes to the true God revealed in his Son Jesus Christ.

René had already heard that Moses received God's Old Testament revelation that God is *I am*, the ground of our very being. And the young man knew that Moses received God's Ten Commandments and hundreds along with that extraordinary revelation. But the young man was only now learning that God revealed in Jesus Christ an even higher revelation than God being life itself. God is love, the highest form of life in that love gives its own life up to the life of others.

The quite limited and dark vision of evolution is that life, whether human, animal, or plant, lives to cast its genes as far as possible into the future in a brute, deadly, and utterly selfish competition for survival of the fittest. And so life might be, were it not for God's infinitely greater revelation. For God knew that to create life only for living would be the ultimately fatal vision, wrapping life in on itself until it had squeezed life out of itself into an eternal darkness.

When God offered not just humankind but all of creation the life of his own Son, his purpose was to reveal that his heart wasn't simply for life but for a special kind of life that continually gives all of itself to redeem and sustain eternally the life of others. Only within that revelation can a beautiful, humane, and good creation exist and prosper.

Yes, God redeemed everything in the gorgeous heart of his humble Son.

René was only beginning to learn the depth, richness, and infinitude of the Word whose Spirit he received as he rose from the Sea of Galilee's waters. But his heart was already telling him that a beginning was eternally enough. His baptism had granted him new life, a new birth that would sustain him eternally.

Moore was thinking these thoughts as he observed the young man seated alongside Eva, enjoying the company of the students as the boat headed back toward the distant shore. Helena's question stirred Moore from his contented reflections. He shook his head.

"No, really, I smell something," Helena repeated, trying to get Moore's attention.

Moore tipped, taking a deep breath of the lake-scented air. He narrowed his eyes, shaking his head once again.

"It smells like an electrical fire," Helena insisted.

And suddenly, with Helena's description, Moore could distinctly smell that very scent. He rose, stepping quickly to the captain's side to share the concern.

Standing at the wheel's console, the captain could not smell anything. But with the boat's forward movement, he could instantly see that only Helena and Moore in the boat's stern might have caught the scent. Leaving Moore at the wheel, the captain stepped quickly to the boat's stern where he, too, picked up the offending scent.

Returning to the console, the captain promptly hit the power switch to turn off the electrical system. The boat's quietly whirring motor and the bluetooth speaker system fell silent.

The students looked back at the captain and Moore, assuming that Moore had decided to let them drift along the waters, hearing only the quiet lapping of the waves against the hull, or perhaps that Moore had a lecture. But no, the captain was already moving quickly toward the small boat's center with a look of concern. Something was up.

The captain quickly cleared the center of the boat's deck, moving students aside. The students lined the two sides of the boat, watching the captain's swift and sure actions. The students could see that Moore had already opened the wheel console to extract the fire extinguisher.

The captain fell to his knees to work open a latch that held shut a hatch in the floor. The hatch hid the boat's many batteries, their wiring, and the electrical system, deep in the boat's hull below the floorboards. The captain struggled at the latch, hurrying to twist it loose, as students watched with wide eyes. The boat had drifted to a stop, so that all aboard could now smell the distinct odor of something burning.

The captain finally worked the latch loose, pulling the hatch open with a jerk. White smoke instantly billowed out, wafting over the students, who moved tighter against the boat's rails, turning away to lean out over the water to try to get breaths of fresh air. Students inhaling the smoke coughed and choked, while other students called to them and tried to help them move to the bow or at a place along the rails for a chance to recover.

The captain, unable to see through the billowing white smoke and into the boat's hold below the floorboards, scrambled back toward the console to retrieve the fire extinguisher. But Moore was already standing over the open hatch, holding the fire extinguisher, ready to send a blast of the extinguisher's carbon dioxide into the hold.

Moore took one quick look at the captain for permission. The captain nodded vigorously. Moore pulled the pin from the extinguisher's handle and squeezed the handle hard. Instantly, a furious emission of angry white CO_2 blasted from the extinguisher's cone-shaped tip, down into the hold. Students covered their ears at the sound of it.

The loud sound and fury of the blast shocked Moore, too, but also reassured him that the device was working. He released the handle. The device's fury instantly stopped. Moore let the white CO_2 drift off, assessing the situation.

Moore's first blast cleared the white smoke from the open hatch. Looking through the open hatch, neither Moore, who stood over the open hatch, nor the captain, who stood alongside, could see any sign of flames in the hold.

"Give it another good blast," the captain said.

Moore bent over, aiming the extinguisher deep into the hold. He squeezed the handle, this time ready for the loud sound and slight kickback of the cloud of CO_2 vapor. The inert gas poured into the hold, choking out any remaining oxygen that might have fed an electrical fire. Students covered their ears again, grimacing at the sound and fury.

Satisfied that the extinguisher had done its work, and not wanting to entirely exhaust its contents, Moore released the handle. Carbon dioxide vapors disappeared into the air. With the boat's electrical system turned off, no spark remained to reignite any offending combustible material. Both the CO_2 vapors and white smoke of the electrical fire had disappeared. Only a slight smell of burned wires remained, hanging lightly in the air.

Falling to their knees alongside the open hatch, Moore and the captain bent over to take another look deep in the hold. Seeing no fire, nor any white smoke, they turned to one another, sharing a high five while still on their knees. The students relaxed in humbled, excited chatter. A few cheered.

"What's next, Captain?" Moore asked, as the two rose to stand alongside the open hatch.

"Give me a few minutes to check things out," the captain replied, as he prepared to lower himself into the hold.

Moore took a deep breath, turning back to Helena as the captain disappeared through the open hatch and below the boat's floorboards.

"A fire on the water, huh?" Helena said quietly to Moore as he took his seat alongside her in the boat's stern.

"René was right again," Moore replied, nodding, as the two of them stole glances at the young man.

René sat alongside Eva, head down, rubbing his hands anxiously. When the young man looked up, Moore motioned to him to join Helena and Moore in the boat's stern. René rose, making his way past the open hatch to join them.

"Thank you once again," Moore said as the young man sat. Moore added, "Your warning helped us prepare. Things might have been different without it."

René nodded. But then looking down at his hands and shaking his head, he replied with a distinct note of sarcasm, "Glad to be of help."

Moore, though, shared a wan smile, saying sympathetically to the young man, "You're understandably feeling a prophet's burden."

René looked up at Moore, sharing the pastor's wan smile while replying, "I hadn't thought of it that way."

"Oh, Elijah, Elisha, John the Baptist, even our Lord Jesus carried heavy burdens when warning of hard things to come," Moore explained.

"And they paid a price for their warnings, didn't they?" the young man replied.

Moore shook his head, answering, "Some did, some didn't."

The young man tipped his head at Moore in interest.

"God carried Elijah straight to heaven," Moore explained, adding in a reassuring tone, "I don't see you paying a price."

René shrugged. He and Moore both opened their mouths to speak, but the captain had emerged through the open hatch. The captain's call to Moore interrupted Moore's quiet consolation of the young man.

"I think I found the issue," the captain hailed Moore.

The captain's call riveted the students' attention. All waited for the captain to reveal the fire's cause.

Suspecting something suspicious, Moore motioned to the captain to join him, Helena, and René in the boat's stern. Moore stood as the captain joined them. Placing a hand on the captain's shoulder, Moore turned him away from the students forward in the boat and drew him in close.

"You found the remains of some combustible material and a peculiar ignition source," Moore told the captain, just loud enough for Helena and René to hear but too quietly for the students to pick up.

The startled captain nodded. He withdrew from his pocket a small, charred receiver.

"I found this in a pile of ashes," the captain said, holding the charred receiver out discreetly for only Moore, Helena, and René to see, while adding, "The ashes looked like they were from shavings, straw, or something similar that someone had dumped over and around the device."

"Or that rats had carried into the hold to make a nest," Moore replied, giving the captain a knowing look.

The captain blinked twice, looking back at Moore while trying to read his intent.

"I have a friend who will be very interested in taking a good look at this device," Moore said, holding out his hand for the captain to turn it over.

The captain paused, still considering. But then he placed the charred receiver in Moore's hand. Moore nodded his thanks.

"My friend will doubtless make a more-thorough investigation of the ashes, probably under the cover of darkness late tonight," Moore resumed, adding, "I hope you'll not mind the unannounced visit."

"You have some interesting friends," the captain finally replied after another pause, this time with a smile.

"Let's hope my interesting friend can take care of your interesting visitor," Moore answered, sharing the captain's smile. He added, "So, how are we getting back to shore?"

"Let's see," the captain replied. Moving to the wheel, the captain announced to the students, "We seem to have burned up a little nest of material. I may have a few wires to change out, but everything looks to be in order."

The captain flipped the power switch back on. A faint hum once again came from the electric motor in the boat's hold. The captain pushed the console's throttle forward, and the boat promptly began drifting silently forward toward shore. The students gave a small cheer, followed by laughter.

"We'll leave that open a little longer," the captain called over his shoulder to Moore, Helena, and René seated in the boat's stern, while pointing at the still-open hatch in the middle of the boat. The captain added with a wink, "Let me know if you smell anything."

Just then, the music popped back on over the boat's speakers, bringing another cheer from the students. Everyone settled in for a pleasant ride back to shore, relieved at having avoided a disaster.

Once back on shore, Helena and Moore shepherded the students back onto the city buses for the short ride back to the hostel, where Helena organized another party to help her shop for dinner fixings at the supermarket across the street. The students had fallen into a satisfying routine, one that allowed them to enjoy the wonders of the Holy Lands even more.

Sitting and chatting with a few students, Moore watched the small parking area behind the hostel, from the hostel's rooftop patio. Soon, a dark sedan appeared. Excusing himself from the students' company, Moore made his way down to the parking lot. Once again, the sedan's rear door opened, beckoning Moore in.

"Here you go," Moore said to the Mossad agent, sitting in the back seat where Moore had stepped in. Moore pulled the charred device from his pocket, handing it to the Mossad agent.

"Thank you," the agent replied, slipping the device into his own pocket while adding, "But we've already got what we need."

Moore raised his eyebrows in surprise but guessed, "So, you had the boat under surveillance and saw who placed the device."

The agent shrugged, unwilling to divulge anything more than he had already intimated with his comment.

"Where do you think the young man stands in this?" the agent asked.

Moore once again raised his eyebrows in surprise, replying almost indignantly, "What do you mean? He's had nothing to do with this."

"His boss does," the agent replied.

Moore's jaw dropped. He leaned slightly in toward the agent, saying incredulously, "You mean, the professor?"

The agent nodded.

Moore sat back, considering the agent's disclosure. Why had the agent even shared this revelation? Moore knew that the agent only shared what would advance the agent's interests, which were the interests of the nation, the security of which he had charge.

"The young man's in trouble," Moore finally said.

The agent nodded.

"What do you want me to do?" Moore asked, knowing that the agent would have some instruction, which would be Moore's signal to leave.

"Let me know the moment the young man shares the next vision," the agent replied, adding ominously, "And watch out for the young man. You, your students, and your friends aren't the targets."

The agent had paused before adding *your friends*, signaling to Moore that he was referring to Helena and Eva.

Moore nodded, turning to open the door and slip out of the sedan. He paused, though, before closing the door behind him. Leaning back into the sedan's rear seat, he asked the agent, "What about the professor?"

"We'll take care of her," the agent said. Not hiding his small smile, the agent added, "Again."

Moore smiled back, nodded, stepped back, and closed the sedan's rear door. He watched as the sedan rolled slowly out of the small parking area and back into the tight alley cluttered with vehicles.

The professor was the title Moore, Helena, and Eva used for the austere figure who had joined them on Moore's prior Holy Lands trip. She had introduced herself as a professor of literature. But she had turned out to be a U.S. intelligence agent, following a dangerous Russian money launderer who was also along, incognito, on Moore's Holy Lands trip.

Mossad had kicked the professor out of the country for pursuing a U.S. intelligence operation in the country without informing Mossad. The Mossad agent had also tricked the professor into turning over to Mossad the Russian whom the professor had arrested in Israel, without having had the lawful jurisdiction to do so. Israel and the U.S. are close allies. Their intelligence agencies cooperate. But intelligence agencies also jealously guard their territory and don't appreciate deception, even by an ally agency.

Eva's special-operations experience on that prior Holy Lands trip had led her to accept the professor's post-trip offer to visit the U.S. agency's New York office, where Eva had accepted a job offer. Moore knew Eva was now a U.S. intelligence agent and that her friend René was also. But Moore hadn't expected the professor to follow them to Israel.

Moore knew he needed time to think. Rather than returning immediately to the hostel, he decided to take a short walk to consider what the Mossad agent's disclosure meant. He headed down the alley and out onto the busy street.

Moore first deduced that if the professor had something to do with the fire on the boat, and maybe even with the kibbutz terrorist attack, as the agent had intimated, and if René was in danger, as the agent had also intimated, then the professor's U.S. intelligence agency evidently wanted to scare, harm, abduct, or perhaps even kill the young man. But why?

Moore considered everything he knew about René. The agency had used the young man as a test subject in mind-control research, when Moore was pretty sure that Congress had long ago prohibited the agency from continuing with that dangerous work. Moore was too well aware of the public reports that the highly questionable fruits of that mind-control work had already fallen into the worst of hands, to the awful harm of innocent citizens.

René, it was clear to Moore, had a growing conscience. His willingness to travel with Eva to the Holy Lands seemed like reliable evidence of it, as did his discussions with Moore and then of course his extraordinary baptism, which seemed genuine. Perhaps the agency saw the young man's growing conscience, and his knowledge of the agency's illegal experiments, as a threat to the agency's relationship with Congress.

But no, Moore thought, that would hardly be enough for the agency to follow the young man all the way to Israel to do him harm. Israel might be a convenient, out-of-country location for the professor to arrange the young man's demise in a way that cast blame on others. Yet the young man's knowledge alone would hardly seem to be enough to condemn him to such an out-of-the-way demise.

Then it hit Moore. René had more than knowledge of the agency's mind-control experiments. The young man also had a capacity for projection or prediction that Moore had never seen. René was a prophet, even if only of his own demise. Could the agency's experiments have given the young man that capability? And did they now want to destroy it so that the young man could not use it against them, even if it meant killing the young man?

Moore soon turned back to the hostel, knowing indeed that he must be extra watchful, and not only for René but also for the students, Eva, and Helena.

As Moore abruptly turned around, an austere female figure who had been following him at a distance ducked into a doorway, just in time to avoid Moore's detection.

14

Moore was up early the next morning, waiting in the hostel's main common room for the first students to join him. No sooner had Moore settled in than Helena joined him.

"Nice to have some quiet time alone together," Helena said with a smile at Moore as she settled in on the sofa beside him.

Moore returned the smile. Helena reached over to squeeze Moore's hand. As she did so, Moore asked her, "How are you holding up?"

153

"Alright," Helena replied, pausing before asking in a slightly strained voice, "Are these Holy Lands tours always this way?"

"What way?" Moore asked in a gentle voice, already knowing Helena's answer.

Helena looked into Moore's eyes. Seeing that he knew what she meant, she waited for his reply.

"No," Moore finally replied with a huff of irony and shake of his head, "No, they're never this way. Except the last two."

"You mean the two on which I've been along," Helena replied with a hint of discouragement.

Moore reached over to gently squeeze Helena's hand, in the same encouraging manner she had just done for him.

"I've been thinking about that," Moore replied, once again gently.

Helena raised her eyebrows and widened her eyes in mixed curiosity and concern.

"No, no," Moore continued, giving Helena's hand an encouraging pat, "It's not you. I mean, it's us."

Helena's eyes widened even further, joined by a tip of her head.

"No, no," Moore repeated again, this time with a wry chuckle and shake of his head, in response to Helena's concerned reaction.

"Well, you'd better explain then, young man," Helena jokingly scolded him, "Or this will be our very last trip."

Moore laughed at Helena's jest before trying again, this time catching and holding her gaze so that she could clearly sense how deeply he felt.

"You know when something very special is going on, how every circumstance seems to want to derail it?" Moore asked.

Helena dropped her gaze, taking a deep breath. When she looked up again into Moore's eyes, her own eyes glistened with tears. So did Moore's eyes.

"The patterns of this world are confused, distorted," Moore explained, "So that when something beautiful and pure arises, the world's patterns immediately work against it."

"And what is this beautiful and pure thing that has arisen?" Helena asked.

Moore reached over, this time turning to Helena to take both her hands. He took a deep breath to answer, but a call from the doorway interrupted him.

"Hey, you two," Eva said in a sleepy but cheerful voice, "I hope I'm not interrupting anything."

Helena gave Eva a mock glare and then laughed. Moore released Helena's hands with a squeeze, drawing from Helena one quick glance communicating, in the best of ways, *this conversation is not over yet.*

"Come on over," Moore invited Eva, motioning toward a seat alongside the sofa. He added, "We need a brief talk."

"Mom's filled me in," Eva replied to Moore as she settled into the soft seat. She added, "Someone set that fire."

Moore nodded but replied, "There's more to it you need to know."

Helena looked at Moore, eyes widening again, this time with a different kind of concern. Catching Helena's glance, Moore pursed his lips, nodding. Looking back at Eva, Moore said simply, "The professor's behind it."

"The professor?!" Eva replied, trying to keep her voice down in the early morning quiet.

"Our friend is watching her closely," Moore continued, trying to quell Eva's alarm.

"Why...?" Eva's voice trailed off, as her mind raced to put two and two together. Moore helped her along.

"René is the presumed target, not you or anyone else," Moore said, realizing that he wasn't necessarily consoling Eva.

Eva looked back blankly at Moore. Moore knew that she was forming the same conjecture that Moore had formed, that René might be escaping the agency's mind-control unit with information or even capacities that the agency did not want René to exploit or share. Finally, Eva spoke up.

"What are we going to do to protect him?" Eva asked.

Moore took a deep breath before answering, "Our friends will handle the professor, as they did last time. We just need to watch closely, listen for René to share anything he foresees, and support René."

Eva nodded. But Helena had a question.

"What about once we leave here?" Helena asked.

Moore nodded. He had been thinking the same thing.

"Let's just agree that René won't be working for the agency," Moore replied, adding, "I've got an idea how to help him, but other things must happen first."

Eva took a deep breath, leaning back in her soft seat, thinking. Students began drifting in, confirming that the conversation of Moore, Helena, and Eva was done. René was among the last to wander in. Moore's thoughts turned to the day at hand.

Moore had planned the students' Sea of Galilee tour with a southern approach that began in Jerusalem, visited Nazareth to the sea's southwest, and then greeted the sea at its southern tip where the Jordan River exits to make its way south to the Dead Sea. Moore then had the students stay in Tiberias, halfway up the sea's western shore, where they boated out onto the sea's middle.

Moore's next plan was for the students to visit two sites farther up the sea, Mount Arbel along its western shore and a Decapolis site along its eastern shore. Both sites had significant gospel connections. Each site would draw the students nearer to Jesus' Galilee home along the sea's northern shore, where their trip would conclude. Moore's tour was drawing them closer to the heart of Jesus, using the geography and history of Israel.

The students were soon on the tour bus to Mount Arbel, barely more than a fifteen-minute drive along the sea's shore, north of their Tiberias hostel. The day had dawned clear. Mist from the sea gave the air a dreamy, shiny presence, making the drive north along the sea's shore even more hauntingly beautiful than it ordinarily is.

The tour bus soon drove past the base of Mount Arbel, rising over the Sea of Galilee. Mount Arbel is the tallest of the mounts and hills lining the sea. Standing atop it and looking to the south, one can see the city of Tiberias stretching from the sea's shore up its own shore-side mount, in a jumble of small, modern buildings. But most of the rest of the vista from Mount Arbel's top is pastoral, very nearly like it may have been when Jesus stood atop the mount.

Moore had the tour bus continue on past Mount Arbel's cliff base, to the north and then west away from the sea, until the bus had circled around the mount to climb to the parking area on its western slope. Moore would walk the students up the Mount Arbel trail to its overlook point high above the sea, where the students could take in the sea's full panorama.

By the time the students had hiked up the sloping trail to the top of Mount Arbel, the sun had thinned the mist rising from the sea below. The students' first sight of the full sea as the trail crested the top stunned them with its beauty.

The eastern side of Mount Arbel falls sharply down a steep cliff face. The students stood at the top of the cliff, looking south to Tiberias from which they had just come and north to Capernaum, where Jesus lived, healed, and taught. Far to the north beyond Capernaum, which hugged the sea's shore, the students could see the snow-capped peak of Mount Hermon on the horizon. Farm fields and vineyards made a gorgeous patchwork of the lush green fields, inland from the sea's shore.

The students stood, pointing out landmarks to one another, occasionally asking Moore the significance of what they saw. As excited as he was at these moments to share the region's biblical stories and significance, Moore knew better than to jump in with long explanations, until the students had drunk in their own impressions, unfiltered by Moore's thoughts and voice. Moore also liked to relive his own first moments atop Mount Arbel, through the students' fresh eyes and innocent hearts.

Moore watched Eva standing alongside René, as the two looked out across the expanse with the same wonder that had captured the students. The young woman had taken the young man by the arm, pulling herself tight alongside him, the first physical embrace Moore had seen the two share. Their solidarity heartened Moore, who suspected that they would need one another in the coming days.

"Good to see, isn't it?" Helena breathed quietly into Moore's ear.

Moore nearly jumped. He hadn't realized that Helena had come so near. He turned to her, though, with a smile and nod, realizing that he wanted to pull her close like the young couple stood, so that the two of them could enjoy the vista together in the same fashion. Moore instead gathered himself, ready to get the students' attention for a discussion.

With the students gathered around, Moore began pointing out the landmarks, just to be sure that the students understood that they were now at Galilee's heart, in Christ's home territory, overlooking the pastoral land where he had chosen to launch his earth-shattering public ministry. The very peacefulness of the region belied the awful cosmic conflict that Christ's ministry would fully and finally resolve.

Moore made sure that the students understood the proximity of Jesus' adopted Capernaum home along the shore below, and the traditional Mount of the Beatitudes site a small distance inland from Capernaum. But Moore also wanted the students to understand the spiritual significance of Mount Hermon, far off on the horizon but still close enough, and with its snow-capped craggy peak dramatic enough, to loom over the pastoral foreground.

Indeed, Moore's primary purpose in gathering the students for discussion atop Mount Arbel wasn't to share geographical information, to identify the biblical sites visible in the brilliant sunlight around them. It was instead to help them see with their spiritual eyes.

Moore began by suggesting, "Mountains are holy places because they are high enough to see the patterns below."

Moore motioned toward the grand vista, not just the beautiful patchwork of fields below and the sea's expanse, but also the heights rising across the sea.

Moore resumed, "When we move nearer God, higher up his mountain, we are not only able to see patterns but also to reckon our way through those patterns, drawing on God's ideal."

The students could indeed make out the lay and structure of the lands in the distance below and all around them. Moore pointed out that they could also see routes and paths through the challenging terrain that they would never have been able to identify if they were not atop Mount Arbel.

"So," Moore continued, "A mountain isn't just a very large pile of rocks, not just a material thing. A mountain is instead primarily a vantage point, the potential for a fruitful ascent, and thus a hugely significant construct that religion itself defines."

Moore looked around to see the students' reaction. Some students nodded, even smiled in recognition of Moore's meaning. Others seemed lost in thought. Moore valued both the nods and the deep thought, wanting the students to open their inner eyes wider to the extravagant, wondrous, enchanted life of faith.

But Moore wasn't done. He then explained to the students that Mount Hermon was the site where many ancient Jews believed, according to the widely read book of Enoch, that the angels of Genesis 6 fell to earth to have giant children with women. Supporting that interpretation, Caesarea Philippi at the base of Mount Hermon was the site of extraordinarily dark pagan worship, at the cave opening known as, and referred to by Christ as, *the gates of hell.*

Moore then suggested to the students that where they stood atop Mount Arbel may well have been where the resurrected Jesus gave the disciples the great commission. Matthew's gospel records that Jesus sent the disciples to *the mountain in Galilee*, for that great commission. Galilee has other mountains, but Mount Arbel is the tallest and the one nearest Jesus' Capernaum home. To Matthew and the other disciples who lived with Jesus below Mount Arbel, Mount Arbel would likely have been *the* mountain to which Matthew's gospel refers.

Moore reminded the students that Jesus declared to the disciples atop the mountain that his Father had given all authority on earth and in heaven to him. In sight of the awful Mount Hermon, Jesus stood atop his own mountain home to declare the cosmic battle over, decided in Christ's favor on the cross, acknowledged and celebrated in his resurrection.

"You are the eternal victors with Christ," Moore concluded, adding, "Whatever challenges you face, whatever hardships you endure, whatever earthly fate befalls you, you will rise in victory with Christ. Let your memory of this place, this moment, and those last words Christ spoke, likely here, strengthen your faith for those times when the battle looks in doubt or even looks lost."

Moore paused, letting the students absorb the moment. He then turned to one of the students with whom he had chatted the evening before on the hostel's rooftop patio, giving the student the signal. The student pulled a small battery-powered speaker from his pocket. Setting the speaker on a prominent rock, the student pulled his cell phone from his pocket to give it a few swipes, until music began pouring from the speaker.

"The Israelites sang songs of victory, just as did the Christians who saw Christ rise," Moore resumed addressing the students. He concluded, "If any of you have favorite songs of victory you wish to play, with which to sing along as you enjoy and explore this vista, please do so."

The students spent another hour atop Mount Arbel. A few wished to explore the caves just over the cliff. Moore encouraged them to do so. A steep trail with many steps led down to some of the caves, maintained for the nimbler and more-adventurous tourists. Moore didn't wish to spoil the students' Mount Arbel visit with a description of the extraordinarily violent history the Jews had endured in and around those caves. Some students were already aware of that history. Others would learn later.

Soon, Moore began gathering the students for their other visit of the day, which would take them around the north end of the sea into the region along the sea's eastern shore that the gospel accounts call the Decapolis and the Gerasenes or Gadarenes. The gospel accounts tell of Jesus relieving a crazed man or men of a legion of demons at that location, after a boat trip across the sea. The demons begged Jesus to send them into a nearby herd of pigs. When Jesus did, the pigs rushed down the hill to drown in the sea.

New Testament scholars do not agree on the precise location of the event, given the only general gospel descriptions of the location. The ancient Decapolis cities of Gadara and Gerasa, to which the gospel accounts appear to refer, were miles from the Sea of Galilee's eastern shore, too far for Jesus and the disciples to have gotten out of their boat and immediately encountered the demoniac or for the pigs to rush down the hill into the sea.

The beautiful hills tumbling down to the sea's eastern shore offer several better candidates for the event. Moore favored one site, modern Kursi, for fitting the gospel descriptions, visually evoking the event better than other sites, and having interesting archaeological excavations. In under an hour, the tour bus had the students there.

Byzantine pilgrims visiting the site in the Fourth and Fifth Centuries warranted and funded significant construction there, including a fifth-century monastery and church, the well-preserved remains of which make for a spectacular site. The students walked up the beautiful cut-stone road to the church entrance, a few magnificent small columns and arches still standing but entirely missing any roof and much of the walls. A few of the spectacular mosaic floors, including one surrounding a baptismal font, survive, depicting local birds, fish, flowers, and fruit.

Once again, Moore reminded the students not just of the site's historical significance and potential relation to the extraordinary gospel event but also of the event's symbolic significance.

The gospel accounts make reasonably clear that the townsfolk chained and tolerated the demoniac at their margins, as they would a scapegoat. The townsfolk could have stoned him to death, but instead they accepted his own willingness to mutilate himself while living among the tombs, as if dead. The demoniac thus contained and held at bay the very evil the townsfolk feared, against which they were quite prepared to enact their own fearsome violence.

Moore pointed out that Christ, as ruler over even the demons, reversed that taxonomy of town violence. Christ freed the lone man of not just one demon but many demons, so that the demons entered two thousand swine that went over the cliff to their death. The many went over the cliff with their many demons, rather than the town casting one over the cliff with his one demon. At Christ's command, the one man then returned to the town to witness to the townsfolk of Christ's rule and healing. Jesus doesn't rule in the world's ways. He reverses the world's distorted patterns, restoring them to the glorious pattern of his eternal kingdom.

The students listened to Moore respectfully until he had finished. They then explored the four-acre excavated site, discovered after the 1967 Six-Day Arab-Israeli War, when engineers attempted to build a road through the site. Extraordinarily, a local monk noticed that the road building was turning up ancient artifacts. He convinced the road builders to stop.

Over the next decade and more, careful excavations revealed the spectacular remains of the ancient monastery and church, the only early Christian presence identified along the Sea of Galilee's eastern shore. Study of the site, its design, and its history indicated its continuous use by Christian until in 741 A.D., an earthquake destroyed the church. Muslims later occupied, repaired, altered, and used the site, leaving modern excavations to sort out the site's Jewish, Christian, and Muslim designs and uses.

Continued explorations of the Kursi site later turned up a nearby ancient synagogue and small Byzantine chapel, alongside a cave and boulder believed to potentially mark the demoniac's tomb-side home.

The ancient church's dark basalt blockwork, set against the white carved columns, enthralled the students with their size, beauty, engineering, and intricate design. The extraordinary mosaics on the church's floor added to the site's wonder, transporting the students far back in time. Moore and Helena watched with satisfaction as the students explored the rich site.

Just as Moore was preparing to gather the students for their ninety-minute return trip to the hostel around the other side of the sea, he saw Eva swiftly approaching, leading René. Something was up.

15

Moore encouraged Eva and René to stroll down the hill for a minute before he caught up with them. They indeed needed to talk. First, though, Moore arranged with Helena to gather the students inside the remains of the ancient church for discussion, song, prayer, worship, or wherever the Spirit led them. Moore would join Eva and René to learn what was up.

Moore found Eva and René seated on an overlook. The serene sea stretched out below them. Mount Arbel stood sentinel across the sea, Tiberias to its south, the Mount of

Beatitudes plain rising behind the seaside Capernaum to its north. Moore paused to take in the scene, before sitting alongside the young couple. Even once he sat, the three remained silent, entranced by the sea's serenity, telling them that the difficult subjects they would momentarily broach already had their settled place in the Lord's grand narrative.

Moore was the first to speak, aware that they might have limited time before needing to meet the students on the tour bus for the trip back to their Tiberias hostel.

"Beautiful, isn't it?" Moore asked.

Eva and René both nodded without removing their gaze from the sea to look toward Moore.

"So, which one of you wants to go first?" Moore asked gently, with a small smile.

Eva and René looked at one another, both seeming to want the other to speak first. Eva finally began.

"We've known the professor had followed us here," Eva disclosed, glancing at Moore to see his reaction.

Moore raised his eyebrows, pursed his lips, and tipped his head slightly, confirming the disappointment that Eva expected. They should have told Moore. Indeed, they had a lot to tell Moore, and Moore knew. Eva continued, first correcting herself.

"Well, she's followed René here. I'm not her concern."

Eva looked at René, trying to decide where to start. But to her relief, the young man spoke up.

"They pressed me to resume the experiments after I'd left the mind-control unit," René said, looking at his hands, trying to say as little as possible while getting directly to the point. But like Eva, he couldn't find the right words.

"What did the experiments require of you?" Moore asked, adding, "And why didn't you want to continue?"

"Both ingesting hallucinatory substances and electrical stimulation of my brain," the young man replied, dropping and shaking his head. Once again, though, he said no more, stuck on the thought.

"How did the substances and stimulation affect you?" Moore asked.

René let out a sharp huff, shaking his head again, before taking a deep breath to reply, "They left me with a heightened awareness of the world's patterns. I can't explain what I felt under their effects other than maybe terror, like seeing what the world truly is."

"And what does the world truly look like?" Moore asked, aware now that René needed Moore to draw him out.

René let out another sharp huff, replying with another shake of his head, "There's a tremendous amount more going on than we usually see."

Moore could tell that the young man was unable or unwilling to reveal more. So he instead turned to the young man's lasting effects from the experimentation.

"So these patterns you now see," Moore resumed, "Is that how you see things coming?"

René nodded, replying, "They seem to point me toward them, like everyone should also see them coming, but they don't. It's terrifying."

"Like the prophets of old," Moore observed, explaining, "They, too, saw the patterns that others should have seen, and it frightened them both to see what they saw coming and to share those warnings with others."

"Really?" the young man asked, glancing over at Moore.

Moore smiled, replying, "Jonah ran from having to share what he saw."

The young man smiled back at Moore, nodding. He'd heard the story of Jonah. But his face quickly grew serious as he asked Moore, "Why are the visions always so dark?"

Moore smiled again, replying, "They're warnings. They don't necessarily come true. Jonah saved a great city with his warning, as reluctant as he was to give it."

René nodded again. Moore continued.

"That's what you're doing. You're warning us of things we should see, that we've given ourselves up to forces we should recognize and reject, turning back to the right path up the right mountain."

René raised his eyebrows at Moore's suggestion. But Moore had a pointed question for the young man.

"What is the professor's intention?" Moore asked.

René jerked his head sharply up at the question. He took a deep breath before replying, "If she can, to abduct me to advance the experiments, but to eliminate me if she cannot."

"And that's why you came to Israel, to get as far away as you could, while enlisting Mossad as your protector," Moore replied, adding, "Not a bad plan, except for one thing."

René dropped his head, knowing that Moore had graciously left unsaid the unfortunate rest, which was that the young man should have considered the danger to the students and others, Moore, Helena, and Eva included.

"I'm sorry," René said, shaking his head, "I didn't think she'd follow me here. But in any case, I should have told you and Eva. You wouldn't have let me join you, but that would have been better than where we are now."

"We'll see," Moore said. He reached over to clap René on the back, adding, "I have a sense things are going to work out."

Moore looked at Eva, asking, "What are your thoughts? What do you see for René and for yourself? I assume neither of you are returning to the agency."

Eva gave a pained smile, exhaling sharply before replying, "You're right about that."

The young woman paused. She turned from Moore to regard René, saying, "Looks like we're in this together."

René looked up at Eva. Each shared a weak smile with the other before Eva added, "I'm not sure we'd be safe in the U.S."

Eva looked at Moore, who nodded. They'd once again been thinking the same thing.

"Let me speak with my friend," Moore said, sharing a hint of a knowing smile with Eva, who smiled back.

Moore later realized that their exchanges showed the value of seeing the world's patterns, both for the short term and long term. René had a highly peculiar capacity to see short-term danger. Moore and Eva had the capacity to see longer-term flourishing. None of the three could predict the future. The future is always uncertain, always potential. But having the Spirit's inner eye for the world's patterns, powers, principalities, and forces gives one a way of navigating more surely and soundly in the world.

Moore took a deep breath, sitting back on the rock on which he had perched to take another look across the sea's waters.

Again looking down at his hands, though, René shook his head, replying, "There's more."

René looked up at Moore, who waited to hear.

"There's about to be an abduction," the young man said, looking straight at Moore but blinking nervously.

Moore looked straight back, asking, "Where and when?"

The young man looked down at his hands again, shrugging and saying, "I don't know. Soon. Could be here, at the tour bus."

René looked up at Moore, adding through tears, "They're taking me, no one else. You'll be alright."

Moore was already rising from his seat and pulling his cell phone from his pocket, ready to swing into action. But first, he reached over to squeeze the young man's shoulder, replying, "No, you'll be alright. Just trust me. Wait here a moment."

Moore stepped quickly away to a secluded spot to make his cell phone call. A minute later, he was back. Eva and René rose to meet him.

"René, I need you to get on the tour bus," Moore said sternly, standing directly in front of the young man to look straight in his eyes. Moore added, "Sit toward the back, out of sight from the front windows. Do not move until I tell you, no matter what you see or hear. Got it?"

René nodded. Moore turned to Eva, saying, "Come with me. We're getting you, Helena, and the students to a secure location."

"Do you think that's necessary?" Eva asked, already following Moore back up the hill toward the excavated ruins where Moore had left Helena and the students.

"We're taking no chances," Moore replied as they hiked smartly up the hill toward the ancient church. He explained, "Another tour bus is on the way. It will be here shortly, waiting for you in the service drive just up the road from the ground entrance. Make your way to it now, following the trail behind the ruins. The bus will take you to the Golan Beach Waterpark, not far north of here. You can spend the rest of the afternoon there, and then meet us back at the hostel in Tiberias."

Another minute of hiking up the hill brought them near the ancient church, where they could see the students gathered around Helena. Moore waved to Helena, sending Eva on ahead to explain.

Moore then turned back to join René at the tour bus. Boarding the steps through the open front door of the bus, Moore greeted the driver, who sat comfortably at the wheel. Moore could see René already seated toward the back of the bus, just as he instructed. But to Moore's surprise, the elderly couple sat with René.

The elderly couple had indeed joined the students for the day's trip, beginning with the Mount Arbel visit. The elderly couple had skipped the kibbutz visit and afternoon on the Sea of Galilee. Indeed, they hadn't felt comfortable joining Moore, Helena, and the students at the Tiberias hostel. They instead got a ride up from Jerusalem to Tiberias only to join the group for the tour's last days.

Moore watched as the elderly couple regaled René with stories and, Moore was sure, more than a little advice. He could see that the couple was keeping the young man at as much ease as was possible for him under the circumstances. For that, Moore was glad. He considered only for a moment sending the couple off with the students on the other bus to the waterpark. But he knew that effort would be useless. The elderly couple would have their own sense of where they belonged. And Moore trusted that they would be right.

Moore settled into the seat behind the driver, to watch out the front window of the bus. The driver turned to chat quietly with Moore, listening carefully to Moore's surprising instructions.

When Moore had finished filling in the driver, Moore stepped out of the tour bus, inviting the driver to follow. Moore and the driver stood outside the tour bus, chatting as calmly and naturally as they could. Moore looked at his watch. They only had to wait. If nothing happened, they'd soon be on their way back to the hostel in Tiberias.

Meanwhile, in the back of the bus, the elderly couple was indeed sharing stories and advice with René, while learning more of the young man's situation.

"So you're Eva's co-worker?" the elderly man observed, to which René nodded

"Strange business you're in," the elderly man observed, adding, "Nothing I could have tolerated for too long, although I suppose it's important that someone does it."

The young man raised his eyebrows at the elderly man's comment but nodded. Picking up on the young man's reaction, the elderly man continued.

"Oh, yes, it's a strange business because it's a strange world," the elderly man explained, adding, "To be dealing with the world's deceptions certainly presents its own hazards, especially when it requires you to be deceptive."

René raised his eyebrows again, this time also tipping his head, once again signaling to the elderly man that his assertions were striking a chord of some sort within the young man. The elderly man chuckled at his own statement and the young man's reaction before resuming.

"Oh, yes, tell the lie, and you become the lie," he said, adding, "And soon, you can no longer tell what's true, fooled by your own deception."

"Now, don't give him too hard of a time, dear," the elderly woman lightly chastised her husband, although only to relieve René of raising his own objection. She actually hoped that her husband would continue. He did.

"Say," the elderly man resumed, as if a thought had just occurred to him, "Maybe that's why you're here, having realized your peril. If so, then you're in a good place, I mean not just the Holy Lands but also with Moore, Helena, these students, and your young woman."

The elderly man chuckled again at his own assertion, especially how he had ended by referring to Eva as the young man's woman. The elderly man saw that he had drawn no reaction from René, who was now just listening patiently and politely. And so, the elderly man resumed.

"I hope you don't mind," he began again, "But my wife and I have wondered about your intentions as to the young woman."

The elderly man stole a glance at René out of the corner of his eye, looking for a reaction. Still seeing none, he continued.

"Too many young men today have no plan, when God's word says that people perish for a lack of vision. If I were you, I'd get a clear vision of my intentions for your young woman. Playing the field does no one any good, especially the two of you."

René shrugged while shaking his head and looking away, silently but clearly indicating that the elderly man had taken far more liberty than the young man expected from anyone. But the elderly man took one last stab at pressing his point home.

"Oh, I know, I know, no one wants to tell a young man anything today," the elderly man, like René, shaking his head and looking away, indicating his own disgust. He continued, "But if I hadn't had someone who cared enough about me to speak to me directly when I was your age, I'd have been lost, likely forever."

The elderly man gathered himself for his final word, saying, "You're in desperate straits, young man, and that young woman of yours is giving her life to help you. If I were you, I'd be giving my life back to her, and swiftly."

"That's enough, dear," the elderly woman scolded her husband, this time meaning it. Pointing forward out the tour bus front window, she added, "And anyway, someone's here to see us."

Indeed, a white van had just swung sharply into the parking lot, pulling to a stop directly in front of the tour bus. René instinctively stood, eyes wide with a wild look and mouth agape. He looked about, as if for a route to run, perhaps to clamor out one of the windows.

"What did Moore tell you, dear?" the elderly woman asked René in a calm voice. She reached over to take his hand, resting on the seat in front of him as he stood, ready to bolt, adding, "Here, let's pray."

The young man looked down at her, helpless. He had only one thing to do, which was to trust, as Moore had asked. He sank slowly back into his seat as the elderly woman began to pray, still holding the young man's hand.

Meanwhile, Helena and Eva had walked the students down the trail away from the ancient church's ruins, not to the public parking lot but to the service drive, where they found a small parking area for the park's maintenance vehicles. No sooner had they gathered there, than the bus that Moore mentioned arrived, ready to take them to the Golan Beach water park.

The students were thrilled to learn where they were headed. They had passed the water park on the way to the ancient ruins at Kursi. Moore and Helena had both heard their excitement, especially among some of the younger students.

Helena hadn't expected that they'd return to the water park for an enjoyable visit that afternoon. She knew that Moore generally avoided tourist sites on his Holy Lands trips, figuring that guests didn't travel halfway around the world for amusement they could find near home. Moore and the Mossad agent, though, had secretly been making contingency plans at each site. The water park was their contingency for any risk that might arise at Kursi's national park.

Helena and Eva put on a good face for the students on the way to the water park and while there for the rest of the afternoon. The students certainly noticed the absence of Moore and René and had questions about the change in buses. But they seemed satisfied when Helena and Eva answered that Moore, René, and the elderly couple were taking the other bus back to Tiberias, which Helena and Eva both hoped and believed to be true.

The water park's rides and grounds, laid out in a beautiful Golan valley stretching down to the Sea of Galilee waterfront, more than occupied the students. When planning the Holy Lands tour, Moore had hoped that he and the students would find occasion for spontaneous fun. So far, the trip had offered ample such occasions, even if they were coming with perils Moore would far rather have avoided.

Back at the public parking lot at Kursi's national park, Moore and the tour bus driver watched the white van enter the parking lot, make a wide turn, and come to an abrupt stop immediately in front of the tour bus, outside of which Moore and driver stood. They both knew that the moment had arrived. They each gave silent prayers that it would proceed as peacefully as possible, without any injury.

Moore watched the white van's driver's door, expecting someone to emerge. Instead, the rear doors of the van flew open. Moore took a deep breath, shot a glance over his shoulder inside the tour bus to be sure things were still in order, and waited for a figure or figures to emerge from the van's open rear doors.

16

The first figure out the back of the white van's open rear doors confirmed Moore's worst fears. The figure wore a mask and carried an assault rifle across his chest in two hands. Scanning the parking lot, the figure swung toward Moore and the tour bus driver, at whom he pointed the assault rifle.

Moore took a deep breath but felt strangely calm in the moment. He'd never had a weapon pointed at him by a hostile figure whose intent he did not know. Instinctually, he recoiled at the event. But deeper inside him, his soul settled into the arms of his Lord.

The figure took a step toward Moore and the tour bus driver, then several steps, the weapon still trained on them. Moore felt instant relief. The figure hadn't opened fire. The figure's intent wasn't to kill everyone in sight. They had crossed the Rubicon. The gambit Moore and the Mossad agent had planned was on.

A second masked figure stepped from the white van's open rear doors, also holding an assault rifle. The figure stood at the van's rear door, scanning the parking lot, while the first figure continued the approach to Moore and the driver standing alongside him, like Moore, preternaturally calm. Moore momentarily wondered whether the tour bus driver had already been through events like this one.

The figure began yelling at the two of them as he drew near, moving the assault weapon in a furious gesture to make the commands clear. As he did so, he pulled a black hood from a pocket with one hand while holding the weapon with the other hand. The figure tossed the black hood on the pavement in front of them.

Moore and the tour bus driver held their hands open and upward, facing the approaching figure, in a compliant but relaxed and firm stance. They each instinctively knew that their body language was influencing the approaching figure, communicating that they, too, controlled the situation. Their actions would dictate the outcome, just as much as the actions of the weapon-wielding figure, perhaps more so.

Moore glanced at the tour bus driver, not knowing the language the figure spoke, which Moore guessed was Arabic.

Without taking his eyes from the figure, the tour bus driver said to Moore, "He says he wants the boy, the young man. He's not pronouncing the name intelligibly, but its your René. And he wants him to come out wearing the hood."

"Tell him I'll get him," Moore replied, adding, "And reassure him we're unarmed."

Moore waited for the driver to relay the message, which the driver did in fluent Arabic. Moore watched the figure's eyes for reaction. The figure's eyes narrowed, and then the figure nodded sharply, once, motioning again with the assault weapon for Moore to retrieve the hood from the pavement in front of him and to get moving.

Moore nodded back, nearly in the form of a small bow, turned slowly, and entered the bus.

Once inside the bus, Moore moved quickly toward the back where René and the elderly couple sat.

"Give me your shirt, quick," Moore commanded the young man, adding, "And your shoes, too."

René opened his mouth to question or object, but Moore, already removing his own shirt and shoes, cut the young man off, saying, "Quick. We have no time to waste."

René hurriedly pulled his light, long-sleeved shirt over his head, tossing it across the back of the seat next to Moore. The young man then slid his shoes off, putting them on the seat.

With his own shirt and shoes off, Moore quickly donned the young man's attire. As he did so, he instructed René, "No alarms. Keep everything normal. It's a delicate special operation. We're not alone."

The young man nodded. Before turning back up the bus aisle, Moore looked the young man in the eyes, saying, "God willing, I'll see you along the north shore tomorrow. Take care of everyone."

René nodded. Moore leaned forward to give the young man a hurried hug.

Turning up the bus aisle, Moore pulled the black hood from his pocket to slip it over his head, pulling its cord snug around his neck as he did so. Steadying himself with his hands on the back of the seat, he made his way blindly and awkwardly to the front of the bus and down the steps, wearing a youthful looking top and youthful looking shoes, every bit like the young man. The black hood covered Moore's head, concealing his true identity from the abductors. The driver steadied Moore as he alighted on the pavement.

As soon as Moore emerged from the bus, the second figure moved smartly from the rear of the van to Moore's side. Taking Moore's arm, he dragged and steered Moore back to the rear of the van and awkwardly up and into, jumping in after Moore and closing the doors. The abduction was accomplished, but so was the gambit. The abductors had the wrong figure and didn't know it.

The other masked figure backed away from the tour bus driver, around the front of the van, and into the passenger's side door beside the van's driver. The van pulled sharply away, wheeling around the parking lot and out toward the national park's exit gate. The tour bus driver watched the van leave. Exhaling sharply in mixed relief for himself, René, and the elderly couple, and apprehension for Moore, he turned and entered the bus for the slow drive back to Tiberias.

René sat stunned, still in the back of the bus, seated by the elderly couple. The driver looked back at the three of them, sharing a shrug and shake of his head before taking his seat behind the wheel, starting the bus engine, and beginning the slow turn out of the parking lot and toward the exit gate.

"Do you know the plans?" René asked the elderly couple in bewilderment, adding, "He said it's a special operation."

179

Both of them shook their heads, the elderly woman replying only, "Trust him."

The young man shook his head in disbelief, asking, "Why is he doing this? He doesn't know what they might do to him."

Shaking his head gently, the elderly man replied, "Oh, he knows the risk. He's just doing as the situation demanded, as our Lord would have done."

"But they'll kill him when they find out they've got the wrong person!" René objected with increasing vehemence.

"They might," the elderly man replied calmly, nodding in agreement, "But that would be no dishonor. He would have done precisely as our Lord did, paying the price for another."

"But it's *not his fault*!" the young man insisted as strenuously as he could without frightening the elderly couple. Tears beginning to stream from his eyes, he added, "*I* brought this on him. *I'm* to blame for putting you all at risk, not him."

"Perhaps so," the elderly man agreed, "Although that conclusion might take much more reflection. But he's still doing exactly as his position requires."

René dropped his head into his hands, bending over on the bus seat while sobbing, "*I* should be the one facing death, *not him*. It's *my fault, not his*!"

"Young man," the elderly woman said gently, as she moved to sit beside him, placing her arm across his bent-over back to give him a hug of reassurance, "God made our world to invite sacrifice. Sacrifice of this sort is the great maker of the world, without which the world wouldn't be the wonder that it is. Moore isn't losing anything at all. He's gaining the greatest possible victory, no matter the outcome we see here."

180

René looked up at the elderly woman. Her words had arrested his sobbing. But her words had shocked him with their new revelation.

"You'll soon see," the elderly woman said gently to the young man, adding, "Let's trust that the Lord has even this awful turn of events in his good hands."

By the time the tour bus arrived at the hostel around the sea's western side in Tiberias, René had composed himself, thinking of the elderly woman's extraordinary words.

The students hadn't arrived yet from the Golan Beach water park, but they soon would. René met them at the hostel's rear door as they piled out of their bus. Putting on a good face, the young man returned their high fives, trying to share in their enjoyment of the late afternoon's recreation.

Helena and Eva were the last to greet René at the hostel's rear door.

"He's inside?" Helena asked René hopefully.

The young man shook his head, taking a deep breath as he did so. Helena shot a panicked glance at Eva before catching herself.

"Let's recruit some help for a quick trip to the supermarket," Helena told Eva, still trying to hold herself together. She added, "The students will be famished."

Eva nodded.

As they went about their way preparing for the evening meal at the hostel, René, Helena, and Eva fielded a few questions from the students about Moore's absence. They answered those questions circumspectly, saying only that he had some business to which to attend.

The students knew that Moore was constantly making, altering, and confirming tour arrangements. Moore also had taken a couple of occasions to renew old Holy Land acquaintances along the tour's way, aside from the students' presence. The students readily assumed that Moore was once again doing so.

The elderly couple joined the students for the evening meal at the hostel, ready to quell any concerns. They had little occasion to do so. They had obtained a hotel in Tiberias for the night so that they could join the tour party for their trip the next day to Capernaum, the Mount of Beatitudes, and the historic north end of the great inland sea.

"Big day tomorrow," Helena reminded the students when the meal had ended, later than usual given the long day of touring, the water park recreations, and the late meal preparations.

The students dispersed, several to their sleeping quarters, some to the rooftop patio to let the late evening linger, and others to the kitchen to help Helena, Eva, and René clean up from the meal. Soon, the clean-up chores were over, and the last few students had drifted away, leaving only Helena, Eva, and René to collapse onto chairs around a small table in a nook off the kitchen.

"Anything more to share?" Eva asked René, hoping that he might have something to encourage Helena.

René shrugged, shaking his head and saying, "He says to keep everything normal. It's a special operation. He'll see us tomorrow along the shore."

"What do you think?" Eva prodded the young man.

René again shook his head, tears beginning to flow from his eyes, while saying only, "He's a very brave man."

Apologizing, the young man rose to head to his room for the evening. Once he had gone, Helena turned to Eva with a question.

"Do you know the plan?"

"No," Eva replied, adding, "Although I suspect it involves the professor."

Helena took a deep breath. Eva reached across the table to take her mother's hand.

"How close are the two of you?" Eva asked.

Helena shrugged, not wanting to think of it. But tears had already filled her eyes.

Eva squeezed her mother's hand, saying only, "It's going to be a good day tomorrow."

The two women rose, hugged, and made their way to their rooms for a long and restless night.

The white van had made a dash north, Moore guessed from the back of the van. The hood covered his head for the entire trip, but the van had seemed to turn right or north out of Kursi national park's gate. From his surmise of the van's speed and guess at the elapsed time, Moore imagined that they were still within Israel when the van stopped at its destination for the night, inside a garage of some sort, it sounded like to Moore.

Moore's abductor sitting near him in the back of the van had conversed periodically with the van's driver and front-seat passenger. Moore did not understand their Arabic, but they seemed reasonably calm. Moore knew that their mood would change soon, in what Moore also knew would be the operation's second critical moment after the initial abduction.

The van's rear door swung open. Moore's abductor gave Moore an Arabic command along with a shove or two that Moore construed to mean to climb out of the van. Once Moore was out, the abductor took him by the arm to steer him forward, back and forth and through several doorways, still blinded by the hood. They soon stopped, the abductor signaling Moore to sit.

Moore listened as figures entered and left the room where Moore sat. Finally, he heard a figure in front of him give a command, after which someone behind him loosened the hood's cord around Moore's neck and pulled the hood off.

Moore sat in a nondescript office, in front of a desk, behind which sat a rough-shaven man with dark hair and light complexion. Moore could see two figures, one to each side of him, and guessed that a third figure stood directly behind him, the one who had removed his hood.

But the four figures were already exchanging animated accusations, pointing at Moore while arguing back and forth. And Moore knew why. He was plainly not the young man they had sought to abduct.

Moore listened and watched carefully, even though he could not understand their Arabic exchanges. He knew that he needed to act at just the right moment, after his abductors had turned their attention from what had just happened but before his abductors had decided on their next action.

Sensing the moment had arrived, Moore began holding up his hands, saying that he had an explanation and *better offer* for them, while pointing to his pocket and signaling that he wanted to make a cell phone call for them to hear his better offer.

Moore's words and actions predictably brought an outburst from the leader behind the desk, who shouted and gestured rudely at his lieutenants. Moore guessed that it was over the fact that he still had his cell phone in his pocket. Moore had been pleased and surprised that they hadn't removed his cell phone, although it wouldn't have defeated his plan. He still would have urged that he make a call for them, using their own devices.

The abductor behind Moore reached into Moore's pants pocket to withdraw the cell phone, tossing it on the desk for the leader to inspect. Moore repeated as plainly as he could that he had a much better offer for them than the young man. He also kept pointing to the cell phone, gesturing that he would initiate the call for the leader to take.

Moore could tell that the leader understood Moore, who suspected that the leader knew English, although Moore's gestures may also have been sufficiently clear. The room grew silent, as the leader looked back and forth from his lieutenants alongside Moore, at Moore, and at the cell phone. Finally, the leader spoke, in heavily accented but easily intelligible English, although in condescending and doubtful tone.

"Go ahead," he said, "Let's hear this offer."

Moore reached slowly forward to slide the cell phone nearer him and turn it around facing him on the desk. He gave it a couple of swipes and taps, until a voice answered in Arabic with what sounded to Moore like a grand and hearty greeting for an old friend.

The call's answer surprised Moore, who had called the Mossad agent. But despite the Arabic greeting, Moore could tell that it was indeed the Mossad agent's voice. Moore resisted smiling with relief both that he had reached the agent and that the agent was wisely greeting not him but the Arabic leader seated across the desk.

Moore watched the leader's response. The leader smiled, then laughed, answering the Mossad agent with a greeting in Arabic nearly as warm as the agent's own greeting. Back and forth their conversation went, at first like two old friends renewing acquaintances but then more seriously, like two old friends negotiating their next arrangement.

Moore was well aware that his Mossad agent acquaintance and the leader seated across the desk from him were in no sense friends. They were instead each key operatives in causes pitted against one another as mortal enemies. But even enemies at times need to communicate in trust with one another, if only to avoid unnecessary destruction of both while advancing, however slightly, their few common interests.

Moore was also aware that the Mossad agent was indeed offering the leader something far greater than the leader had anticipated in attempting to abduct René. A market exists between enemies for their prisoners. Nations and factions trade prisoners, in simple or complex swaps, based on the values the parties assign to the exchange. Some prisoners have greater value than others. Money, technology, sanctions relief, safe passage, and other things of value to abductors and their sponsors have their own value in prisoner exchanges.

The Mossad agent knew that the professor and her U.S. agency had offered the leader something in exchange for abducting and either killing or handing over René. But the Mossad agent conjectured that the young man had only a modest value in the exchange, or the professor and her U.S. agency would have chosen a more-skilled, better-resourced, and more-prominent leader for the abduction. So, the Mossad agent upped the ante, offering to hand over something of far greater value to the leader.

Moore had a guess as to what the Mossad agent might be offering the leader, although only a guess. Because the conversation was in Arabic, he couldn't tell the terms. But Moore could see from the leader's growing smile, and the nodding encouragement of the leader's lieutenants, that the leader was warming to the offer. Indeed, when the conversation ended, it was clear to Moore that the Mossad agent and leader had struck a deal.

"Let us make you comfortable tonight," the leader addressed Moore in his heavily accented English, adding, "Your friend and I have some business tomorrow, of which you will be a part."

The leader smiled at Moore. Moore nodded, while giving a small bow forward in his seat, in a gesture of gratitude and respect for the transaction of which Moore's own life was now a part.

17

The next morning dawned clear and sunny again, like every other day the students had enjoyed in Israel. The students knew that they would be spending the day around the adopted home of their Lord Jesus Christ, in Capernaum and its environs. They also knew that their tour was on its homestretch and that before long, they would return to their own earthly homes, carrying more of the Lord's Spirit to share with their friends and families back home.

Helena, Eva, and René welcomed the students to breakfast as they drifted into the dining area. René had risen uncharacteristically early, the first rather than the last to enter the kitchen and dining area. He already had coffee brewing and breakfast fixings out on the kitchen counter when Helena and Eva joined him.

"Get any sleep?" Eva asked René, being sure to put her hand atop the young man's hand as he leaned on the kitchen counter.

René smiled, nodding and replying, "More than I expected."

Eva could see a change in René, one that she hadn't expected overnight, especially such a difficult night wondering and worrying about the welfare of Moore. But the change Eva noticed in the young man was one that she had desired and one that she welcomed, despite its unusual timing.

To Eva, René looked conscious, aware, as if an inner eye had awoken within him. In Eva's reckoning, René had always been kind, intelligent, and even gentle and sensitive. But Eva had never quite felt that the young man was alive inside in the manner that she somehow expected and surely desired, both for him and for her.

Throughout the trip, Eva had been thinking about the young man's condition, how he seemed to encounter and move in the world. Perhaps it was the influence of the Holy Lands, or maybe it was the students of faith surrounding them, but Eva had come to discern that René was absent from his own interior, robbed in some way of his own spirit.

Eva had initially ascribed the young man's shallowness to his situation, that he was effectively on the run from an experience and an organization that had the capacity to destroy him. But Eva had soon come to conclude that the young man's inward poverty was instead an issue of his spirit, not of his situation or emotions.

The young man's growing openness to faith, across the Holy Lands sites and the conversations they generated, had greatly encouraged Eva. His slow spiritual awakening was exactly that for which Eva had hoped and prayed. The young man's surprising baptism had thrilled Eva. Yet she wondered whether and when she would discern a maturation and transformation in the young man's abiding spirit.

Eva had heard and seen that the Spirit sometimes comes before the outward markers of faith, like conversation, confession, and baptism, while sometimes coming after those outward markers, as the New Testament accounts themselves reflect. Yet this morning, watching René move about the kitchen and dining area, beginning to interact with the sleepy students as one by one they joined them, Eva felt that René had indeed received his transformation. She only hoped it would endure what might prove to be a difficult day.

When Helena soon joined them, Eva immediately picked up that her mother must have noticed the same difference in René that Eva had noticed. When Helena joined the young man and her daughter in the kitchen early that morning, she greeted them each with a light hug, the first time she had included the young man in that warm gesture she usually reserved for her daughter.

"Looks like you managed some sleep last night," Helena quipped at René with a smile after their brief, light embrace.

René nodded, returning Helena's smile and replying, "And you? I didn't expect a restful night for any of us."

Helena shook her head lightly. Not wanting to remember the night, she tried quickly changing the subject with the first thing that came to mind, saying, "Any dreams last night?"

The moment Helena said it, she realized how awkward and inappropriate her question was, with all that René had been through. Eva, too, jerked her head up from her breakfast preparations to watch the young man's reaction.

But René just smiled. Indeed, he emitted a light chuckle, replying, "Yes, in fact. I hadn't remembered it until you asked."

Helena and Eva both looked at René, waiting for him to share his dream, as he recalled it. He chuckled again before he began, not with any look of concern or horror, as Helena and Eva feared, but instead with a growing smile.

"We were all on a sunny hillside overlooking the sea," the young man began. He paused to pull the details back from his subconsciousness, checking the coffee maker as he did so.

Helena and Eva looked briefly at one another to see what each was thinking. Eva raised her eyebrows slightly, tipped her head, and shrugged, drawing a small smile from Helena, before René finally continued.

"Other things were going on that I can't quite recall," René related. He narrowed his eyes, looking up to the left while struggling to make out his dream's strange order, before adding, "You and he, though, were together among us. Something was going on between the two of you that caught our attention."

René paused again. Helena glanced at Eva, puzzled. Eva caught her mother's glance, not with puzzlement but with a small smile.

"You mean Moore?" Helena finally asked, quietly, trying not to interrupt the young man's effort to recall his dream's details.

"Of course," René replied, hardly hearing Helena's question, before adding, "You know, I think he was proposing."

René chuckled again, shaking his head in amusement while turning away to fuss with the coffee maker, oblivious to the responses his disclosure had engendered. Eva snickered gleefully while Helena blushed, giving her daughter a mock glare of chastisement.

Moore, like René, had a surprisingly restful night. His abductors kept a close watch on him within the structure to which they had moved him. But he was given a room with a bed, permitted to use a bathroom, and given food and drink. As far as Moore could tell, his abductors stationed a guard outside the door to his room. But he wasn't going to attempt to escape even if they had not. He remained a key part of the coming transaction the Mossad agent had offered and the faction leader had accepted.

When morning came, Moore's abductors fed him breakfast, even bringing him thick coffee. Moore didn't know the timing or specifics of the coming exchange. He only knew that he needed to wait patiently.

Sitting alone in the room, its windows covered but hints of bright daylight peeking through the covering's cracks, Moore might have thought of himself. No one would have blamed him if he had. But he strangely had no concern for himself. He instead thought of René and Eva. Would they be safe if they returned, the Holy Lands trip over, to the U.S.? Was remaining in Israel instead an option? Should their future be together? Or was it only circumstances that had thrust and held them together, such that they would grow apart when their current common challenge resolved?

As Moore thought of the young couple, he paused frequently to listen, consider, reflect, and pray, not yet looking for answers but instead to ensure that his heart for the two of them aligned with the heart of God. If Moore had a role in guiding them, counseling them, even making or soliciting arrangements for them, God would soon tell.

Moore's thoughts also turned to Helena. He had thought of her so often, considering, remembering, reflecting, intuiting, trying to discern where her best future lay. Moore recognized his interest in her but gave that interest fully away, relinquishing it into the hands of God. He would not let his interest stain his prayers for her nor his will that she should prosper in the path that God alone arranged.

Moore thought of the item he held in a small case in his pocket, there in the event that God spoke again what Moore had been hearing from his Spirit for some time. He generally trusted that he could discern the Spirit's movement, always consistent with the word of God. Yet he knew well enough that when the Spirit seemed to nudge him toward his own desires that he must wait for the clearer sign. He would in this case put out the fleece of Gideon, waiting for God's sign.

As the morning hours in the still, dark room passed, with no sign of action yet outside, Moore fell not into worry or despair, not into doubt and questions, but into a reverie that he only rarely experienced and never deliberately sought. Moore had read the counsel of the ancient church fathers, some of them hermits and mystics, not to directly pursue the divine, nor to pay attention to one's own rare reveries. Should they come, accept them. Should they go, let them go. Speak of them seldom.

Moore slipped from the side of the bed on which he sat, to kneel on the floor, at first turning to rest his head on the bed, but when that posture seemed too proud, to turn again to lower his forehead fully to the floor. In that humble posture, his heart continued to swell to meet the divine.

The effect of the experimental hallucinogens the professor's U.S. agency had given René is to radically increase the brain's neural connections. The drugs' effect can be to so flood the brain with visions the wild connections generate, as to drive the user mad. We survive and navigate in the world not by taking more of it in, as the internet's madness invites, but by limiting its flood to manageable portions. Our madness today is limitless connections. Those who draw not madness but prophecy from the hallucinogens are fortunate to have brains capable of fruitfully limiting the otherwise deadly flood.

In his humble reverie, spawned not by hallucinogens but instead by a simple purity of soul, prompted by unusual circumstance, Moore experienced no fruitful visions. He simply accepted the flood of God's loving grace, pouring profusely out of his Son's magnificent sacrifice with which God made, ordered, and redeemed his world.

Not far to the south from where Moore patiently awaited his fate, assured of its fruitfulness, the tour bus headed north from Tiberias the short distance to Capernaum, hugging the Sea of Galilee's northern shore.

Capernaum, or Kfar Nahum as locals identify the spare village today, was the Lord's adopted home, what the New Testament accounts refer to as the Lord's *own city*. Jesus moved to Peter's shoreside Capernaum home, after Christ's own townsfolk drove him from Nazareth, nearly throwing him over a cliff when he announced his ministry in his home synagogue.

Capernaum was not only Christ's base for his travels throughout the region for the three years of his public ministry. The Lord also worshiped, taught, and did miracles in Capernaum, making it the Galilean center of his unprecedented ministry. If Jerusalem was the final stage for Christ's full revelation as the sacrificed and resurrected Lord of all, then Capernaum was his chrysalis, his transitional stage from youth and young adulthood into history-changing King of kings and world-rescuing Savior.

In the seaside Capernaum, a fishing village of about 1,500, Jesus chose the fishermen James, John, Peter, and

Andrew, and the tax collector Matthew, among his first and leading disciples. But in Capernaum, Jesus also raised Jairus' daughter from the dead, healed the Roman centurion's servant, and rid a possessed man of his demon. And in Capernaum's synagogue, Jesus preached his sermon that he was the bread of life, among the regular messages he gave there.

The students had three Capernaum sites to visit, each tucked right up against the seashore. The tour bus parked at the Kfar Nahum national park, where the students could walk through well out on a pier to enjoy the north Sea of Galilee vista in the cool morning air. The students lined the pier, from which they could see southwest past Mount Arbel all the way to Tiberias, and to the east and southeast to the Golan Heights hills tumbling down to the sea's shore. Helena, Eva, and René watched the students from the shore.

The elderly couple, who had rejoined the tour party for the ride north, waited on the tour bus, saving their energy for later sites. The national park site does not include Capernaum's excavated and preserved treasures. Those treasures instead lay just to the southwest on a plot of seaside land that Franciscans bought in the 19th Century, on which to build a monastery preserving the ancient Capernaum sites. Helena, Eva, and René soon directed the students back to the tour bus for the short drive around to the monastery grounds, taking them past a lovely and historic Greek Orthodox Church along the seashore between the national park and Franciscan monastery.

The students poured out of the tour bus again, across the monastery grounds, to explore the excavated ruins of an ancient Capernaum fishing village. Helena, Eva, René, and the elderly couple joined them, strolling slowly through the ruins, while watching the students explore. The sun was already warming the rocks cut and stacked into the ancient remains of low walls, outlining small residences and storehouses along narrow lanes.

As small as Capernaum was in the days of Christ's earthly ministry, the village had an outsized significance as a trading post along the prominent Via Maris, or Way of the Sea. Travelers from as far away as Babylon and Syria, and between Egypt and Damascus, would pass through Capernaum, along the edge of the life-giving inland sea.

Capernaum didn't exist as a city in Old Testament times. Its population rose only a couple of centuries before Christ's advent. The city lasted well more than a thousand years before its demise as a trading post and return to a quaint fishing village. The synagogue in which Jesus worshiped and taught fell a couple of centuries later, replaced by another synagogue, the remains of which the Franciscans preserve to this day. The students wandered among the synagogue's few remaining columns and walls, marveling at their designs and inscriptions.

The site's main attraction for the students, as for most visitors, lay among the ruins of an octagonal church, sheltered by a modern octagonal structure inviting visitors to stand over the church's remains. A glass floor in the modern structure permits visitors to look down on a small room in the center of the ancient church's ruins, believed to be the remains of Peter's own residence, where Christ lived during his public ministry.

Helena and Eva had visited the site with Moore on their prior Holy Lands trip. They knew that the provenance of Peter's presumed residence included its ancient modification from a small home to a slightly larger place of Christian worship, in the century or two after Christ's ministry. They watched as the students gazed through the modern structure's glass floor at the tiny ancient church, imagining what it might have been like to worship there, where Christ had eaten, laughed, consoled, maybe wept, and slept. The elderly couple took seats on a bench along the modern structure's glass wall, soaking in the students' wonder.

After having given the students the chance to examine and reflect on the tiny room and nascent church, Helena stepped forward, asking if the students would like to commemorate their visit with their own brief worship. The site's host had welcomed Helena's request to do so, pointing out that it would continue the Christian worship at the site that had begun two thousand years earlier.

Helena invited the students to begin with a song of their choice. *Amazing Grace* was their consensus choice. Calling up the hymn's lyrics on cell phones, they began:

Amazing grace! how sweet the sound,
  That saved a wretch; like me!
I once was lost, but now am found,
  Was blind, but now I see.

'Twas grace that taught my heart to fear,
  And grace my fears relieved;
How precious did that grace appear
  The hour I first believed!

The Lord hath promised good to me,
  His word my hope secures;
He will my shield and portion be
  As long as life endures.

When we've been there ten thousand years,
  Bright shining as the sun,
We've no less days to sing God's praise

Than when we first begun.

The song having concluded, Helena invited a prayer. Eva volunteered. Students bowed their heads as the young woman first thanked the Lord for his life and ministry, and then called upon the Lord to bless and protect the students, give them hope and a future, and draw them near. Her heart prayed silently for Moore, a silent prayer in which Helena and René joined.

As Eva concluded her prayer, Helena looked up at the students gathered around, asking if anyone had anything more to say. She was just about to dismiss the students after a respectful pause, when to her surprise René spoke up.

"Permit me, as the least and last among you, to say these few words," the young man began. All heads turned toward René as he continued.

"The humblest Lord ever to live, who chose his home in the tiny, dirt-floored, rough-stone-walled hovel beneath us, has called us to live as he did."

René took a deep breath, searching for the fewest words with the greatest truth and impact, before continuing.

"He asked that we die, welcome our burial, and then embrace our resurrection in him, to live as he did, not for himself but sacrificially for others, and in so doing to receive immeasurable and eternal treasure."

René paused again, thinking of the man whom God had chosen to lead him to this conclusion, before he resumed.

"When Christ offered us this path, he revealed the fundamental principle on which he made and organized his world, that of a sacrificial love that frees the soul for the glorious destiny he designed it. I wish to thank our Holy Lands host Moore for teaching me this truth of all truths and pray for Moore's eternal reward for his unending and profound witness."

René stepped back and turned, indicating that he had concluded. Students nodded, then clapped, a few even cheering respectfully, as much as the octagonal modern structure's decorum seemed to permit it.

The impromptu worship over, the students dispersed across the grounds to explore the ancient village's preserved ruins. They would soon be on their way to the nearby traditional site of the Mount of Beatitudes, just uphill and inland from Capernaum.

Other events were already developing at the Mount of Beatitudes site, having very much to do with Moore's future.

18

Moore's abductors entered his room, tossing the black hood on the bed beside where he sat on its edge, motioning to him to don it once again. Moore complied. His hour had come.

Led blind once again through the abductor's safe house, Moore arrived back at what he presumed was the white van. Into its rear compartment, he climbed once again, to sit along one of its panel walls on what felt like a low bench. Momentarily, the garage door opened, and they were on their way, Moore hoped to the arranged destination.

The day before, Moore had been surprisingly non-anxious, almost serenely calm, even though his fate had then been significantly more uncertain. Now that his abductors had accepted the Mossad agent's offer, though, and he was now on his way to what should presumably be his escape from harm, Moore was far from serene. He instead felt at odds, maybe even worried and confused.

Moore chalked his tension up to having no further active role in whatever outcome he faced. He was now a pawn, someone else's pawn to move, whichever way circumstances took him.

As Moore came to that conclusion about his confused state, with the van trundling around curves, tipping the blinded Moore this way and that way, Moore huffed to himself in appreciation for the conclusion's irony. Had he ever been in control? Wasn't God always his protector and provider? Moore reminded himself that just because he felt helpless, his fate entirely in the hands of others, shouldn't mean that he relinquished his faith.

Finally, though, the van came to a stop. When its driver turned the van's engine off, Moore could make out voices in the van's front seat, speaking in Arabic.

A U.S. embassy vehicle soon entered the parking lot, at the far end of which sat the white van. The embassy vehicle parked a safe distance away. A slender, austere, female figure emerged from the front passenger door of the embassy vehicle, standing alongside the vehicle to cautiously assess the white van through dark sunglasses, worn against the midday sun's bright glare.

Carrying a slender briefcase stuffed with U.S. currency, the female agent made her way at a deliberate pace across the parking lot, dotted with a few cars. As she neared the white van, the van's rear doors opened, and a masked figure stepped out. The masked figure held up an arm, inviting the female agent to step into the rear of the van to inspect its human cargo. As the agent stepped into the van, the masked figure relieved the agent of the briefcase, shutting the van's rear doors to stand outside of them, patiently holding the briefcase.

Back across the parking lot, just as the white van's rear doors closed, a dark sedan pulled silently up alongside the embassy vehicle, blocking the embassy vehicle's occupants from their view of the white van. A male agent leaped from the embassy vehicle's rear door to admonish the sedan's driver to move the vehicle out of the way. The agent left the embassy vehicle's rear door open.

No sooner had the male agent moved to the sedan driver's window to gesture and shout at the driver, than the sedan's rear door opened sharply, blocking the agent from returning to the embassy vehicle. The agent spun, ready to slam the sedan's rear door shut to protect the embassy vehicle.

But the Mossad agent, Moore's contact, had already stepped smartly from the sedan's open rear door, blocking the embassy agent from shutting the rear doors of either vehicle.

Holding up his credentials, the Mossad agent smiled at the furious embassy agent, saying, "I'll only be a minute. Wait here."

And with that, the Mossad agent slipped into the embassy vehicle's rear seat, closing the rear door behind him. The embassy agent stood outside the embassy vehicle's locked rear door, glaring at the Mossad agent inside.

"Good day, Ambassador," the Mossad agent greeted the U.S. ambassador seated alongside him in the rear of the embassy vehicle, adding, "Good to see you again."

The ambassador narrowed his eyes. Trying to be sure he had identified the Mossad agent correctly, the ambassador replied, "You're the one who conspired with that American pastor to trick us into giving up the Russian to you."

"Yes," the Mossad agent replied with a shrug and small smile, adding, "And you're the one who violated international law and interfered with my country's sovereignty in secretly arresting the Russian within our borders."

Both the ambassador and Mossad agent had just spoken truly. Moore's prior Holy Lands tour had ended with exactly that result. Moore had helped the Mossad agent recover the Russian from the U.S. embassy, in a ruse they had planned and executed together.

Meanwhile, inside the rear of the white van, the female agent stood over the hooded prisoner with the boyish shirt and shoes, sitting on the small bench alongside the van's panel wall. A second masked figure stood alongside the female agent in the van's rear, holding an assault weapon to guard the prisoner. The masked figure holding the assault weapon gave a command in Arabic for the female agent to remove the seated prisoner's hood.

The female agent loosened the hood's cord around the prisoner's neck and pulled the hood slowly up.

As the hood rose over his eyes, Moore looked up into the female agent's eyes, greeting her, "Good day, professor."

Back in the embassy vehicle, the Mossad agent was explaining to the ambassador an offer he should seriously consider.

"The terrorist faction that abducted your American pastor has just exchanged him for your female agent," the Mossad agent began.

"What do you mean?" the ambassador replied with a sneer, "They abducted our young male agent. We're just getting him back to conduct him safely back to our soil."

"No," the Mossad agent corrected him, "They abducted your American pastor, and your intention wasn't to return your young agent to your soil but to eliminate him."

"What do you mean, *eliminate him?*" the ambassador sneered.

"Oh," the Mossad agent replied, "Am I putting that too indelicately for you? That was simply how the terrorist whom you hired to abduct him described your transaction."

The Mossad agent took a deep breath, shaking his head and blowing air sharply out his lips, ready to end the conversation.

"Call your agent in the rear of the white van," the Mossad agent suggested, adding, "And explain to her that you will soon be arranging the swap of their faction leader, whom you hold back in the U.S., for her, likely in an African location where these things usually occur."

"Why, you are negotiating on behalf of terrorists!" the ambassador accused the Mossad agent in a rage.

The Mossad agent shook his head, calmly replying, "I have negotiated nothing other than the release of your American pastor, abducted in a transaction you arranged and financed. If that abductor has now taken a different agent of yours than the one you intended them to eliminate, then that's not my problem, even though I have just conveyed to you their solution to this problem you created."

In the rear of the nearby white van, the stunned professor looked down at Moore with narrowing eyes, saying nothing. Moore continued to look back up at the professor, knowing that her mind was racing through the possibilities of what might have happened to bring them to this point and what might happen next.

Before the professor could get too far with whatever contingency she might have planned, Moore suggested, "Why don't you give the ambassador a call?"

The professor narrowed her eyes further but reached slowly into her pocket with her free hand. Her other hand still held the black hood she had removed from Moore's head, expecting to see her young agent René one last time, to confirm his identity before completing the nefarious transaction.

As the professor reached for her cell phone, the masked figure pointed his assault weapon at her and stepped behind her to stand between her and the van's closed rear door. The professor slowly pulled the cell phone from her pocket, ready to give it a swipe and tap. But to her surprise, her phone was already ringing.

"Yes, ambassador," the professor said after tapping the phone and raising it to her ear.

While the professor listened on the cell phone, Moore rose slowly from his bench and stepped aside. The professor sank slowly onto Moore's bench seat, still listening to the ambassador on the cell phone. A moment later, the call had concluded. The masked figure took the cell phone from the professor's hand, slipped it into his breast pocket, and barked an order in Arabic to the professor, who, taking one last glance at Moore, slipped the hood onto her head.

In another instant, Moore was out the white van's rear doors. The masked figure standing outside handed Moore the briefcase, jumped into the rear of the van, and closed the doors behind him. The van immediately started up and pulled away, leaving Moore standing alone at one end of the parking lot, holding the briefcase.

Shielding his eyes against the bright sun, Moore took a look around the parking lot, instantly recognizing where he was. He was in the parking lot of the Church of the Beatitudes, at the traditional location of the Lord's Sermon on the Mount, atop a gentle hill overlooking Capernaum and the bright blue Sea of Galilee.

Moore scanned the parking lot for the familiar dark sedan. And there it was at the other end of the parking lot, alongside an official-looking vehicle. A buff-looking male figure in a plain gray suit stood between the two vehicles, eyeing Moore. Moore sauntered over, carrying the briefcase.

Inside the embassy vehicle, the Mossad agent waited patiently for the ambassador's brief cell-phone conversation with the professor to end and for the white van to roll by on its way out of the parking lot. He then turned to the ambassador for his parting comments.

"I'm glad we were able to free your American pastor," the Mossad agent began, adding, "I can see that here he comes now, looking well."

Indeed, the two of them could see Moore strolling calmly toward their two vehicles, raising a kindly salute of greeting to the brooding male agent standing between the two vehicles.

The ambassador said nothing in reply. The Mossad agent shrugged, turning to exit the embassy vehicle's back seat. But just before opening the rear door, the Mossad agent turned back to the ambassador.

"Oh, and one more thing," the agent said, "You'll be leaving the young man alone. Consider him now under our auspices and good care."

The ambassador took a breath and opened his mouth to reply, but the Mossad agent had already turned away, opened the door, and exited the vehicle in a swift and lithe motion.

"Moore!" the Mossad agent hailed the pastor as he neared, while ignoring the male embassy agent glowering behind him.

"Oh, wait a moment," the Mossad agent apologized to Moore, holding up a finger to stall Moore's return greeting.

The Mossad agent turned back toward the embassy agent, giving him a small jerk of his head to indicate that the embassy agent should get in the open rear door of the embassy vehicle. The embassy agent complied with one last glower. As soon as the embassy agent had shut the embassy vehicle's rear door behind him, the Mossad agent gave the embassy vehicle a double slap atop its trunk. The embassy vehicle's driver dutifully started the vehicle and pulled away. The Mossad agent watched the embassy vehicle slip out of the parking lot and down the long driveway to the exit of the church grounds.

The Mossad agent then turned back to Moore with a broad smile of satisfaction, saying with a small shake of his head, "I do love this job sometimes."

Moore laughed.

"So, are you alright?" the Mossad agent asked Moore.

"Couldn't be better," Moore replied with a relieved smile and nod.

"We've arranged for your young man's safety here in Israel," the Mossad agent said, adding, "Although we can't promise anything elsewhere."

Moore nodded, saying only, "Thank you. I have some ideas, but it's up to them."

Moore looked down at the briefcase hanging from his hand. Raising it up, he asked the Mossad agent, "What do you want me to do with this?"

"Let's call it the young man's severance pay," the Mossad agent replied with a smile, adding, "It may take a while for his former employer to process his separation paperwork."

"Done, then," Moore replied, after sharing a good laugh with the Mossad agent. Moore added, "Are visas available for the two of them, if they choose to stay?"

"I'll arrange it," the Mossad agent replied. Extending a hand to Moore, the agent added, "Need a ride?"

Moore shook the Mossad agent's hand firmly, shaking his head and replying, "No, I think my ride will be here any minute."

Moore paused for a moment before adding with a smile, "Unfinished business, you know."

The Mossad agent laughed, nodding and slapping Moore on the shoulder, before turning with a half wave to get back into the dark sedan. Moore watched the dark sedan glide quietly from the church parking lot and out the exit.

Moore had many sites across the Holy Land that he could call his favorite, after one manner or another. The Church of the Beatitudes site was certainly one of those, perhaps somewhat more of a favorite than other favorites. As Moore stood in the parking lot, believing that he might have a few minutes or even an hour or two before his happy tour party arrived to join him, Moore remembered why the site was a favorite of favorites.

Moore turned from the exit drive, running up the mount on which the grounds sat, in the downhill direction, south over the top of the church grounds and toward the great inland sea. And there, nestled deep among the surrounding hills, the sea sat, its blue shimmering in the midday sun.

Moore took a deep breath, breathing in not just the sweet, dry air, lightly scented by the orchards and vineyards surrounding the rocky church grounds, but also the view of the inland sea and its sheltering hills, across which the Lord had laid his life, its teachings, its healing balm, and its salvation. Moore was home, at the Lord's feet, soaking up his Sermon on the Mount and absorbing his very life along with it.

Picking up the briefcase at his feet in the parking lot, Moore strolled from the parking lot, surrounded by rocky scrublands, up the walkway and into the church's courtyard. The courtyard was filled with lush plantings and shaded by swaying date palms, a marvelous hillside oasis tucked into the dry hillsides.

The Church of the Beatitudes is a modern structure, constructed in the mid- to late-1930s, in a neo-Byzantine style, honoring the spare ruins of a tiny late-4th Century Byzantine church just downhill from the modern church. Those ruins, assumed to venerate the Sermon on the Mount site, include indications of an ancient cistern and early monastery.

The Roman Catholic authorities funding and constructing the modern church gave it an octagonal design, commemorating the great sermon's eight beatitudes, or supreme blessings. Moore stood at the chapel's entrance, imagining what it might be like to pastor there, baptizing infants and adults, sharing communion, and marrying. Thinking of that last sacrament, Moore instinctively felt his pocket for the small case he had kept there throughout the Holy Lands tour.

Moore wanted to stand at the parking lot, watching for his party's tour bus to arrive. But the Spirit instead called him onward, further into the church complex. He picked up the briefcase at his feet to walk around the little chapel and to the sheltered veranda, looking through columned arches down to the great inland sea.

The moment his eyes saw the sea, Moore recalled that this vista from the church's veranda was his favorite of favorites, topping even Mount Arbel's extraordinary view of this church grounds and the whole of the sea. Setting the briefcase at his feet, Moore stood, staring silently out across the sea, wanting the moment to last and linger, even though the moment also held such great anticipation.

Helena, Eva, and René had finally gathered the students from the Capernaum village grounds, ushering them back to the tour bus for the short ride uphill to the Church of the Beatitudes. The elderly couple had already made their way to the bus to sit and rest, waiting for the students to join them.

As the tour bus made its circuitous way up to the traditional site of the Sermon on the Mount, Helena was unsure of what to expect next, how long they would be without their tour party leader Moore, and if and when he would reappear. Her only indication from René was that they were to continue on as planned, expecting that Moore would rejoin them when able. René had nothing else to share.

The tour bus reached the parking lot of the Church of the Beatitudes within a few short minutes. The students piled out, lured forward from the dry, warm, and bright parking lot, toward the oasis holding the lovely neo-Byzantine church. Helena, Eva, René, and the elderly couple followed, as the students explored the grounds, examining its plaques, inscriptions, statuary, and paintings, and enjoying its flowers, fountains, and pleasant sights and sounds.

Helena paused at an old stone fountain, listening to the water gurgle down from the spout to the pool below. Eva and René wandered on ahead, while the elderly couple caught up to Helena, stopping to enjoy the fountain with her.

"How are you holding up?" the elderly man asked Helena, while the three of them watched the water tumble down the side of the stone fountain.

Helena shrugged, glancing at the elderly man with a weak smile of gratitude for his concern. She really didn't know how to feel. René had told her nothing other than that Moore would rejoin them as soon as able.

"Your Moore is quite a hero," the elderly man replied in answer to Helena's shrug.

Helena glanced again at the elderly man, slightly raising her eyebrows in interest. The elderly woman gave her husband a warning glance that the elderly man either missed or ignored.

"To give himself up to the abductors in the young man's place, that was a Jesus moment," the elderly man continued, incautiously, for Helena was now exhibiting more than curiosity, more like alarm.

"I'm sure he had a plan," the elderly man rambled on, adding, "I'll be glad to learn it when this is all over."

The elderly man's words stirred a flood of bewildering emotion in Helena. She raised her hands to her mouth, trying to compose herself, trying to hold back the tears that had wanted to burst forth from the first moment she had learned from René that Moore was absent.

The elderly woman glared at her husband, admonishing him, "Now see what you've done. You should have left well enough alone."

Seeming to notice Helena's alarmed reaction for the first time, the elderly man said, "Oh, my, I can see how I've upset you. Tell you what, there's a peaceful spot just around the chapel on its veranda, where you can collect yourself with the most beautiful view of the sea."

The elderly man stepped aside, motioning to Helena to make her way in the veranda's direction, while his wife glared at him, preparing to give him the rich tongue lashing he deserved.

The elderly man watched with a small smile as Helena moved off toward the veranda, hands still held to her mouth, trying to contain her emotions.

The elderly man's wife opened her mouth to begin to give her husband his sorry due, but looking at her, he held a finger to his lips to shush her, whispering with a mischievous look, "Wait. You'll see. He's here, on the veranda."

The elderly woman stared at her husband, her fury slowly turning to relief and then joy. A great smile spread across her face as she buried her face in her husband's chest, the two of them embracing in a long hug.

Soon, though, the elderly woman pulled back to ask her husband, "Why did you have to give her such a hard time, telling her of Moore's abduction?"

"She didn't know the depth of his sacrifice for the young man," the elderly man replied, adding, "She needed that revelation of his character."

Still holding her husband around the waist, the elderly woman poked him in the chest, saying, "A sacrifice you once made for me."

19

Helena reached the chapel's veranda, her teary eyes fixed on the mesmerizing beauty of the sea, made all the more beautiful by the view through the veranda's columned arches. But she gave a start when she noticed a figure's movement just down the veranda, a figure she hadn't immediately noticed because of the sea's allure.

It was Moore. He had turned to see who had joined him to soak up the sea's peace, so like the comfort of his Lord. Moore smiled at Helena. Helena buried her head in her hands, rushing to Moore, who caught her in a long, close embrace. The two stood as one, rocking one another back and forth in joy and relief.

Helena finally pulled back from their embrace, saying through tears, "I didn't know.... I wasn't sure...."

Moore shook his head in sympathy, gently shushing Helena with the reply, "I didn't know either. I didn't mean to worry you. But it's over. We're together. We're here."

Helena sniffled an acknowledgement, nodding and repeating, "We're together here." Yet she then looked up in Moore's eyes, asking, "But what does that mean?"

Moore raised his eyebrows slightly, while giving a slight tip of his head, repeating, "What does that mean?"

Helena laughed nervously through her sniffles. Looking down at her hands, which had found Moore's hands, she replied with another chuckle, "René dreamed we married."

"How did you feel when he told you that?" Moore asked, looking down at Helena, who still looked down at their knitted hands.

Moore had his permission in the young man's dream. But he also needed Helena's permission.

Helena tipped her head this way and that, shrugging and giggling through her sniffles, unable to look up at Moore or fashion a suitable reply in her blushing embarrassment.

Moore, though, read Helena's response according to her unexpressed wishes. Still holding Helena's hands, he slowly bent to one knee so that he was now looking up at her, into her lowered eyes. As he did so, Helena began to weep, happy tears of outpouring emotion.

Freeing his hands, Moore reached into his pocket to pull out the little case he had carried for days through the Holy Lands, waiting for God's will and the will of the woman weeping before him to conjoin. The moment had finally come.

"Will you marry me, my Love?" Moore asked, still kneeling, while holding up and opening the small case before Helena to reveal a glistening engagement ring.

Helena wept and nodded, nodded and wept, wiping tears and giggling all the time. Moore stood, pulling the ring from its little case to slip it awkwardly on Helena's bare ring finger of her left hand. The two then embraced again, a long, happy hug, out of which they finally turned together to look out through the columned archway to the gorgeous sea beyond.

"Our moment," Moore said, as the two stood side by side, holding one another around the waist, looking down the mount to the glistening sea.

"Our moment," Helena repeated, finally composed, settled in her spirit, but now filled with the joy of a new life and new adventure.

With their one commitment, their one step into each other's arms, both Moore and Helena indeed had a clear path and new purpose. Everything that had been so uncertain for each of them, so unclear and unfinished while alone, had suddenly been drawn taut, like an arrow shot through their hearts, pointing them together toward their Lord.

Some engagements raise more questions than answers. Some engagements turn two lives, each already of clarity and purpose, toward uncertainty and a looming question of undefined potential. Other engagements take two wandering souls and send them together into a new wilderness, still without a path to the promised land on the other side. Yet a few engagements come with a clear path for the new couple to follow, when their paths alone had been unclear, uncertain, and undefined.

Engagements don't have to be perfect. Some engagements work because they introduce new chaos and its fresh potential into the staid lives of individuals whose identity had grown stale. That's the tendency of the one, to harden into its own limits. Yet the tendency of any two is to stir the hardness of the other into a fresh new hue. Every engagement forecasts a new color, the unique mixture of two formerly stale hues.

The elderly couple, Eva, and even René had known that the engagement of Moore and Helena could make a beautiful new color. Each, though, had wisely waited and trusted that God alone would reveal whether he favored that new hue.

Moore and Helena were still looking out under the veranda's columned archways at the sea below, arms around one another's waist, when Eva, René, the students, and finally the elderly couple joined them on the veranda. Neither Moore nor Helena moved. They simply greeted the others with a nod and smile, inviting them to share the moment and view.

Eva joined her mother at her side, putting her arm around her mother's waist, to look out across the waters. Helena smiled at Eva before returning her gaze to the sea. René joined Moore at Moore's side, putting an arm over Moore's shoulder. They exchanged knowing smiles before returning their gaze to the sea. The elderly couple stood under the next columned arch, likewise arm in arm, looking out across the water. The students let their tour party leaders enjoy the moment, as they, too, gathered on the veranda, looking out across the water.

"Looks like you two have something to share," Eva said quietly to her mother, glancing at her mother's new ring.

Helena tipped her head back and forth while sharing another smile with her daughter, sensing that the news was Moore's to share. Helena looked up at Moore, smiling. When Moore met her gaze, Helena nodded, granting him that permission.

"Students, friends," Moore called, as he turned from Helena's side to address the gathered party, "Thank you for letting me finish some other business over the past twenty-four hours. I trust that you enjoyed the water park yesterday afternoon and Capernaum this morning. I'm sorry I was not able to accompany you."

Moore paused, gathering his thoughts, thinking not of himself but of the students and of Eva, René, and Helena.

"You've been a great group," Moore resumed, "And this trip has easily been my most memorable. We have just one more day to explore this northern Galilee region. Tomorrow, after a restful night back at the hostel in Tiberias, we'll visit Chorazin and Gamla, significant sites that I'm sure you'll appreciate."

Moore paused again, looking at Helena with a big smile. Helena pursed her lips and put her hands on her hips in mock irritation at the obtuseness of Moore's address. Moore laughed at Helena's silent warning. Having amused her just as he intended, Moore resumed.

"But Helena and I first have a little news to share with you. Helena didn't know it, although she might have guessed, but I invited her on this Holy Lands tour to propose to her, if it worked out, on this very spot."

Moore gave Helena another broad smile, adding, "It worked out. She has accepted. I hope you'll celebrate with us tonight back in Tiberias."

Eva gave Helena a great hug, while René gave Moore a hearty handshake and the students cheered, surrounding Helena and Moore with congratulations.

Soon, the students began to disperse, making their way slowly back through the grounds toward the tour bus. Eva drifted off with Helena, who looking back over her shoulder gave a wink to Moore, drawing from him another big smile. René followed Eva and Helena.

Moore, though, called René back to where Moore still stood on the veranda. Moore bent down to pick up the briefcase, still at his feet. Holding it out to René, he said, "Here, from the U.S. government, a down payment on your severance pay."

René raised his eyebrows, regarding the briefcase but not yet taking it from Moore's hand.

Moore smiled, explaining, "Blood money, in a way. The professor gave it to the abductors. Our Mossad agent friend arranged to get it back for you."

"And the professor?" René asked.

"She's presently indisposed," Moore replied, adding, "While your former agency arranges her release. Our Mossad agent friend felt it appropriate that she should stand in for you with the abductors she arranged."

René nodded, eyebrows raised in surprise and appreciation. Moore lifted the briefcase up to the young man once again who, after another moment's pause, took it with a deep breath of its figurative weight.

"That's not all," Moore resumed. Putting a hand on the young man's shoulder, Moore added, "Our Mossad agent friend gained your former agency's commitment to leave you alone, at least on Israeli soil. You and Eva will have visas available, if the two of you choose to stay here."

René looked down, nodding and replying, "Thank you. I'll share it with Eva to see how she feels."

"Share with her how you feel, too," Moore advised the young man, adding, "And not just about the visa offer but also about her, will you?"

218

René gave a slight chuckle, looking up at Moore with a nod and weak smile, and replying, "Probably high time that I do so."

The tour party was soon back on the bus to the Tiberias hostel. On the way, Moore, sitting beside Helena in the front of the bus, filled her in on the Mossad agent's offer that René and Eva remain safely in Israel.

"What do you think of the offer?" Moore asked Helena.

"What do you think they would do here?" Helena asked Moore in reply.

"I have an idea," Moore answered, "But I want to see what they say first. René wouldn't give any indication until he first spoke with Eva."

"Wise young man," Helena replied with a sly smile and playful poke at Moore's ribs.

Moore chuckled, nodding.

The tour bus had the party back at the hostel in short order. Moore stood outside the bus door, clapping each student on the shoulder or sharing a high five as they made their way off the bus and into the hostel.

The elderly couple were the last ones off the tour bus. The elderly man pulled Moore aside, saying quietly and with a warm smile, "My wife and I have the privilege of making dinner arrangements for all of us tonight, for a true celebration. Is *Little Tiberias* okay with you?"

Moore raised his eyebrows in appreciation, replying, "Wow, that's entirely unnecessary but much appreciated. Helena and I were going to run over to the supermarket for dinner fixings for everyone."

"Now, that's no way to treat your new lady on the day of her engagement," the elderly man good-humoredly scolded Moore, adding, "Then *Little Tiberias* it is," referring to a popular restaurant for fine dining, serving local fare.

In an hour, the whole party had gathered at the restaurant, ready to celebrate not only the engagement of Moore and Helena but the whole trip, the students' growth, and their upcoming return home. Eva and René had their own new liberty to celebrate. The evening turned out to be magical, a glad communion stoked and warmed by the party's several major life events.

Early the next morning, Eva and René met Moore and Helena in the hostel's nook just off the kitchen, where Moore and Helena had already made coffee and begun breakfast preparations for the students. Moore's mind was already turning to the trip back to the sea's northern end for visits to Chorazin and Gamla. Eva and René, though, had made other plans.

"If it's alright with you two," Eva proposed to her mother and Moore, both of whom sat at the nook's small table, eager to hear Eva's proposal, "René and I have a visit in the other direction to make."

Moore and Helena glanced at one another, each wondering what Eva and René had discerned. Yet each also wanted Eva and René to explore, assess, pray, and decide their next steps of their own accord, not based on the counsel of Moore and parental advice of Helena, certainly not at their direction.

"That's fine, Honey," Helena said brightly after a respectful pause to give Moore a chance to opine otherwise.

"May we meet you back at the college tonight?" Eva asked the two of them.

Once again, Moore and Helena shared a quick glance before each nodded to Eva, Moore adding, "Sure, just let us know the moment you need anything."

No sooner had Moore and Helena agreed, than Eva and René nearly jumped up from their seats at the small table to say goodbye and head for the hostel's door, outside of which they had a ride waiting. Moore noticed René stop just long enough to grab the briefcase he had stowed discreetly near the door.

"So, what do you think is up?" Helena asked Moore once the young couple had left.

"I figured you'd know," Moore replied with a smile.

"I think we've both got a good guess," Helena answered her brand new fiancé.

Moore nodded, taking Helena's hand to give it a light squeeze.

"So," Helena continued, "They're making plans. Should we?"

Moore laughed, replying, "Oh, that's right. We've got some discerning to do, too. Tell you what. We've got a long last day here in Israel to lead and enjoy. How about if we spend the flights back tomorrow doing some serious planning?"

"You're on, Mister," Helena said in mock seriousness, adding, "And until then, I'm not letting you out of my sight."

The students were soon up, fed breakfast, and ready to embark for their last day of exploration. The tour bus awaited them outside.

Moore tried to make it a point to include a visit to Chorazin in each of his Holy Lands trips. While Jesus lived in Capernaum during his public ministry, he preached throughout the region, very likely including in nearby Chorazin, just inland a short walk from Capernaum, and nearby Bethsaida. Indeed, the gospel accounts make clear that the citizens of all three adjacent, north Galilee towns, constituting what we oddly call today the ancient *evangelical triangle*, rejected Christ's teaching. Christ condemned his adopted hometown Capernaum, and Chorazin and Bethsaida, for rejecting his word.

Moore had that reason for including Chorazin on his tours, that Jesus very likely taught there. But Moore had two other reasons for taking the students to Chorazin. One was to see the well-preserved ruins of a Second Century synagogue there, adjacent to the even older ruins of a synagogue where Jesus may well have taught.

For Moore, the black-basalt stone synagogue ruins at Chorazin gave more of the material context for those who first heard Jesus preach in the area's synagogues than any other site. The students were able to observe the size and general configuration of the synagogue's basilica meeting place, its ceremonial mikvah bath, the Moses seat where the synagogue leader sat, the chief seats for the synagogue's scribes, and even the Torah closet storing the Hebrew Bible scrolls.

Moore also appreciated the synagogue's black basalt, quarried locally, giving the synagogue a distinctively North Galilee look. The ornate decorations the ancient craftsmen carved into the massive columns, stones, and furnishings further made the site a classic one to visit for impressive ruins.

But the other reason Moore wanted the students to see the ruins of Chorazin had to do with Christ's prophecy of its demise. Today, Capernaum, Chorazin, and Bethsaida are hardly an evangelical triangle. Although bustling population centers in Christ's earthly day, they are today ghost towns, abandoned to nothing but spare ruins of their ancient life and commerce. Excavations around Chorazin show its repeated destruction, sometimes by earthquake, notably in 360 A.D. as the bishop historian Eusebius recorded, and other times by military conquest or merely by abandonment.

Moore wanted the students to have a physical representation of the spiritual lesson that our life is in

Christ. Those who reject him will find instead their inevitable demise.

Moore had a similar reason for taking the students on to Gamla, further west on the Golan Heights, after their Chorazin visit concluded. Gamla was not likely among the towns in which Jesus commonly preached. It was a prominent Seleucid-Greek city, not a Jewish settlement, before late in the First Century A.D., when it became a key home to the Hasmonean Jews. The gospel accounts make no mention of Gamla. Its location further up into the surrounding hill country and more distant from the Sea of Galilee, would also not have made it a convenient preaching site.

Gamla instead makes a popular tourist site because of its dramatic location at a strategic point along the heights, at which one can just catch a glimpse of the Sea of Galilee in the distance. Gamla is also a popular tourist site because of the large size, complexity, and well-preserved nature of its ancient ruins, including fortress walls, residences, and a large synagogue. Gamla is finally a popular tourist site because of the dramatic battles that took place there during the *Great Revolt* of the Jews against Rome that eventually led to the 70 A.D. destruction of Jerusalem's Temple.

Moore explained to the students who had hiked with him up to Gamla's fortress heights that we know a great deal about Gamla's battles because the Jewish-Roman historian Josephus had made Gamla his garrison home when Galilee's Jewish commander. Gamla's residents were sympathetic to the Jewish refugees who began to take shelter there in the hills above the sea, from the Roman forces. Josephus soon garrisoned the city, joining the stone houses around its perimeter into great fortress walls, while using the steep hills and ravines for natural protection from the thousands of Roman soldiers.

Moore shared with the students that Gamla eventually fell to the Romans after successive sieges, leading to the deaths of thousands of Jews. Remarkably, Josephus survived execution, instead taken in by the conquering Roman general whom Josephus' wit somehow entertained, to advise on Jewish affairs. Josephus wrote the famous Roman history *The Jewish War*.

Moore further reminded the students that Josephus also wrote the *Antiquities of the Jews* in which he recorded his own account of Jesus the Messiah, a wise teacher and miracle worker whom authorities crucified. Josephus wrote in the same history of John the Baptist. Anyone demanding independent historical sources for the life and ministry of Jesus Christ, outside of the many New Testament manuscripts, must deal with Josephus.

For Moore, Gamla, as much as any other location in the Holy Lands, thus bears its own peculiar witness to the Messiah, that Gamla's Jewish-Roman commander would write a pagan history acknowledging the Messianic claim of the miracle worker Jesus. For Moore, Gamla also bears its own tragic witness to secular political and military affairs, that one can never fully appease the military general nor please the political king.

Moore's students left Gamla sobered in their faith, for the tour bus ride back to Jerusalem and the college, to pack for their plane flights out of Tel Aviv the next morning.

20

Helena and Moore had settled into their seats for the flight from Tel Aviv to London, where they would make their connecting flight to Chicago. The students were spread in seats all around them. Helena and Moore could see a few chatting with one another, excited for the trip home. Others, they could see, had already fallen into the stupor that all would soon assume, exhausted from the travel and trying to get some rest for the reentry at home.

Missing from their group of intrepid air travelers returning home, though, were Eva and René.

Helena and Moore waited until their flight was in the air and had climbed to cruising altitude, before they began the conversation they each knew they wanted and needed to have.

"Feels strange without them," Moore observed.

"You mean Eva and René?" Helena asked, drawing a nod from Moore.

"Do you think they made the right decision?" Helena asked, drawing another nod from Moore, tempered by a tip of his head back and forth.

"Hard to know what the future holds," Moore observed, "But they're in a good spot for now. What do you think?"

Helena nodded.

Eva and René had taken the day before, the tour party's last day in the Holy Lands when Moore and Helena took the students to Chorazin and Gamla, to visit Kibbutz Degania again at the south end of the Sea of Galilee. Helena and Moore hadn't heard, but on the tour party's first visit to the kibbutz, Eva and René had agreed how idyllic it would be if they lived and worked on the kibbutz.

Their return visit to the kibbutz the day before had garnered them an invitation. It is not unusual for a kibbutz to accept short-term and long-term guests. Some guests, Americans included, visit for a month. Others, intending to visit for a month, stay thirty years. The visitors may bring children, skills, or simply labor. All share in the work of the kibbutz, whether the traditional farming or modern tourism or industry. All receive in return the same small stipend, plus food and board.

Eva and René had rejoined Moore and Helena at the college in Jerusalem at the end of that day, to tell them their exciting news. If they had the blessing of Moore and Helena, then they intended to accept Kibbutz Degania's invitation to remain in Israel. They would teach, cook, serve, and offer the kibbutz whatever other skills they had, including greeting American tourists, tourism being one of the kibbutz's productive offerings.

The kibbutz's interest in desalination, hydroponics, and other technological advances had also intrigued Eva and René. They foresaw offering the kibbutz their services in adopting and improving technologies, and advancing their business, management, and communication systems. René had engineering training and skill. Eva was a technological whiz.

René had made the kibbutz one other offer, indeed a gift. Eva and René had returned to the college in Jerusalem without the briefcase. Although the contents of the briefcase were in a very true sense his due, René had no intention of retaining those contents. If their visit to the kibbutz had accomplished nothing else, the young man's gift of the briefcase and its contents would have been more than enough to justify the visit. How the kibbutz applied the substantial funds was up to the kibbutz, no strings tied.

Moore and Helena had instantly understood and appreciated the young man's gift, indeed applauded it. They also understood and appreciated the young couple's plans to spend an indefinite period integrating themselves into kibbutz life.

"René needs to heal," Moore suggested to Helena. He added, "I can think of no better place to do so than the kibbutz."

"And they need time to get to know one another in a healthier setting," Helena offered, adding, "They shouldn't base a relationship on rescuing one another from a bad situation."

Moore and Helena thus agreed that Eva and René had accomplished everything they could have hoped for and more, in undertaking the Holy Lands tour. They had received and embraced every gift of the trip, the greatest gift being the Spirit's blessing of new faith.

"I'm kind of envious of them," Helena lamented, watching Moore closely for his reaction.

Moore huffed, smiling weakly while nodding and replying, "Sure seems to simplify life."

Helena looked at Moore, assessing his mood, listening to the Spirit, waiting to discern whether she should speak and, if so, what she should say.

"What would you think if we joined them?" Helena finally asked, still looking straight at Moore, hoping that she could trust him to dream with her.

Moore looked back at Helena, first with a straight face, making his own assessment of how serious Helena might be and what were her feelings and intentions. Gradually, though, he smiled, drawing a smile from Helena.

"Sounds like a dream, doesn't it?" Moore asked, drawing a broader smile and nods from Helena.

"A simpler life, the past left behind, a new beginning in a beautiful land, waiting for us to further explore," Moore resumed, trying to discern and list the things that had encouraged Helena to suggest it. He continued, "A chance to continue to help and enjoy Eva and René, not to leave them completely alone in a challenging new place and time."

Helena nodded with each of Moore's suggestions. Soon, though, the two fell silent, thinking of both the wisdom and challenges of Helena's idea, and how they might move in that direction if their discernment was that it was their right path.

Finally, Helena spoke up on the other subject they knew they needed to broach, saying, "How would that dream fit with our wedding?"

Moore smiled broadly, even chuckled lightly, replying, "Exactly. Our wedding plans might be very different, depending on the life we plan and pursue together."

Helena thought for a moment before asking with a serious, questioning look, "Were we foolish to put marriage before even thinking of how we would fashion a life together?"

Moore smiled wanly. Shaking his head, he took Helena's left hand, the one having the finger with the engagement ring on it, to give it a light squeeze.

"No," Moore answered gently, continuing to shake his head, "I can't see doing any planning together without the commitment first."

"Did you want me to join you in your pastoral ministry?" Helena asked, again with a serious, questioning look. When Moore looked down in response, at their two hands still clasped, Helena took it as a signal to add, "I would, if that was your desire."

Moore looked up at Helena with an appreciative smile, replying, "I know you would, and your willingness means a lot to me. But I don't know whether that is our path."

"How do you think we find out?" Helena asked, giving Moore's hand a squeeze.

"I think you've hit on exactly our answer," Moore replied, explaining, "We should take our time listening to one another and our own hearts, while sharing our engagement news with our communities, who may help us in our discernment."

Helena nodded. After a moment's further pause, she smiled, adding, "So, no need to plan the wedding date and place yet, until we have a direction together, whether in America or Israel?"

Moore nodded, sharing Helena's smile.

"But I'm not letting you go," Helena teased Moore.

"Hey," Moore replied, in the same teasing vein, "*I'm* the one who should be worried."

They both had a good laugh. Soon, they each tipped their heads back, relaxing for the long flight, while still holding hands.

Three months later, Moore was on the reverse London to Tel Aviv connecting flight.

Having returned to their homes, Moore and Helena had soon realized that indeed, they each needed a new start. Moore's congregation was glad for his engagement and ready to welcome Helena as their pastor's wife, as soon as the nuptials had occurred. Helena would have dutifully served, just as she had promised Moore. But Moore couldn't see it, whether because he had once served the congregation with his dear, departed wife or because he just needed a fresh start.

Helena had a similar experience with her own small circle of friends in her own community, distant enough from Moore's home as not to have any intersection with it. Helena's friends were delighted for her and would have welcomed Moore, whether he had been a pastor, politician, or pauper. But Helena couldn't see it, whether because she had once enjoyed those friends with a different husband beside her or because she, too, just needed a fresh start.

And then, both Moore and Helena had come to realize that they had stronger commitments to the Holy Lands and the young couple who resided there, Eva and René, than they any longer had to America. America had once been their home, in every sense of the word. Yet it now no longer felt so, in any sense of the same word.

Moore spent greater time than Helena exploring that question of why things had changed so much that he felt closer to a distant land halfway around the world than to his own birthplace. Moore knew some good reasons why that was the case. He was pastoring in a very different society than the one that had raised him and supported his call to ministry.

But rather than find the reasons for his willingness to leave his homeland in personal history, marital loss, vocational maturity, social change, spiritual malaise, or political reform, Moore decided to treat it as a matter of the soul. He figured he now had less time remaining on earth than he had already enjoyed, perhaps much less time. God could call him heavenward tomorrow. Why not spend his next years letting God draw him closer while he was still here on earth, before his final journey home?

Moore wanted to let God strip his life of worldly things, especially positions and possessions and their distracting concerns. Moore wanted instead to nurture relationships, with Helena, with Eva and René, with whomever else God cast in his path, and with God himself.

Moore and Helena felt ready to join Eva and René at the Kibbutz Gedania, where Eva and René had prospered. Eva and René had grown close. Helena believed that they would soon announce their engagement. Indeed, Eva had urged her mother to join her and René for a visit and to stay as long as she wished. Helena had the sense that Eva and René had found a home and wanted their family to join them, perhaps even to help raise their own children soon to come.

Moore had encouraged Helena to go for an extended visit and to report back. Almost immediately, Helena had urged Moore to join her at the kibbutz on whatever shorter or longer terms he could arrange. She had even suggested that they marry in Galilee, at whatever location Moore preferred, although she mentioned the Church of the Beatitudes chapel, which had been Moore's first thought as well.

And so, Moore had approached his elder board with a proposal for a sabbatical study. The kibbutz would make a perfect home to learn more about Jewish life, history, and culture, while exploring the Holy Lands to learn more about the earthly home of the incomparable Lord. The board had granted Moore three months away, all of which Moore intended to spend with Helena in Israel. They would make their wedding plans once Moore had arrived and settled in at the kibbutz.

Well on his way on the final London-to-Tel Aviv leg of his trip, Moore began to doze off. And as he dozed, he dreamed, not of fires and abductions, nor of other torments, but of the gorgeous Sea of Galilee, about to become his temporal home, as it had forever been his spiritual home.

Milton Keynes UK
Ingram Content Group UK Ltd.
UKHW020629200524
442968UK00001B/31

9 798892 928625